Crows
And other Pedestrians

Rita Traut Kabeto

Crows and other Pedestrians

Text and illustrations by Rita Traut Kabeto
Cover design by Rita Traut Kabeto

copyright 2011 Rita Traut Kabeto.
ISBN 978-0-9635416-2-8
published by Rita Traut Kabeto

Contact: Kabetofandr@gmail.com
Website ritakabeto.com

Contents

Feudal America

My insurance company just upped my premium again. It has done this every year since we bought our home – automatically, no questions asked, and no apology. I told them that since my employer had not automatically raised my wages that I was not able to comply with the insurance company mandate for a higher premium. Actually, I no longer receive wages at all because my employer moved to a new location, and the pollutants at the new site affected my health. I was sixty-five, so I retired.

A mandate it is. I was told that the higher premium was to offset the rise in the value of my home. In re-figuring the premium, though, my agent admitted that part of the raise was not due to the increased value. It was just for nothing, or for company profit, or just for fun – who knows. He could not explain it.

I pointed out to him that since the value of my home, modest as it is, would probably rise every year, consequently, the premiums would also rise. But where would it end? The day would come when I would be required to pay thousands of dollars, while I have trouble paying the premiums right now. Oh no, my agent said, the premiums would eventually level off. When? He didn't know. Could he guarantee it? Of course not.

In an effort to come to grips with this problem I asked to simply insure the house for a lower value. After all, my fire department is just blocks away and there are two fire hydrants in the immediate vicinity of my home. A fire would surely be put out quickly and would do only minor damage. One hundred thousand dollars would certainly pay for repairs. That was not permitted.

Then I checked with the bank that holds my mortgage. How about just insuring the money that is owed to the

1

bank. I have higher-power connections and will feel quite safe without complete coverage. No, that cannot be done. And because the house is over one hundred years old, albeit just recently totally remodeled, with proof by local and state authorities that plumbing, wiring and all other items involved in remodeling are up to code, they could not provide homeowner's insurance coverage at all. Could not, they said. Would not? I queried, for other companies will insure my home. Would not, the bank admitted.

The number of insurance types is staggering: property insurance, mortgage insurance, auto insurance, medical insurance, life insurance, disability insurance, flood insurance, nursing care insurance, funeral insurance, and probably a few others of which I'm ignorant. And all this insurance is disguised as reassurance against disaster later on, which may or may not happen, while it pinches us so thoroughly right now and every day, that mandatory costs hover like a black cloud over our lives.

The peasants and serfs of past ages must have felt the way I do right now. They were dominated by their masters who called all the shots, had all the rights, had all the power, and the poor peasant had to deliver or die. Actually, the poor peasant often delivered and died anyway because not enough was left for him to sustain himself and his family. American corporations have become the feudal lords of the 21st century, and they differ from the earlier ones only by a better disguise of their milking practices.

Adding insult to injury, these feudal lords squeeze us till it hurts, pay themselves outrageous wages and bonuses, then use some of our stolen money for charitable purposes. In other words, first, they prevent us from having a better quality of life by milking us through mandatory costs, then they feed us some of the stolen money as charity and garner thanks to boot. But even these charitable ventures are pure self-interest for they keep us in that economic twilight zone where we still have a little something to lose and are thereby kept from starting a revolution.

Our 21st Century feudal lords have more than one way of milking us. They manufacture products that are not needed, then pay the advertising media for creating a need by skewing our value systems to fit the new product. Some of the most blatant distortions of real needs are created by playing on our fears of getting sick, namely the cleaning – sanitizing – of everything we touch and breathe. Room spray – how about opening the windows? Air sanitizers – open a window! Bathroom deodorizers – open the window! Upholstery spray – open all the windows, often! Even inside the refrigerator they spray, and right under the baby's nose to sanitize the highchair tray, claiming, of course, that there is no risk to the baby and its lungs. If these sanitizers were needed to keep us well, the generation that created this perversion would not exist because its parent generation would have died long before it was old enough to procreate.

To ensure ever more profit for corporate America, the advertising media creates for us, almost imposes on us, totally new standards of living and being, aimed at getting us to buy what the feudal lords want to sell. An old man I used to know once admonished me, on leaving the house on a rainy day, to walk between the drops. He was joking, of course, but I have learned to do just that: walk between the drops. I do this by choosing my own path and not feeding into that which corporate America and its advertising media declares that I should have, or be, or do. I don't buy sanitizing spray – I open my windows.

The other day I came across a TV commercial in which CEOs and employees of a large corporation were overjoyed for having reached a new high level of achievement. Since profit making is the priority and bottom line, I fear that they have discovered another, more perfect way of squeezing more money out of us. It's scary.

Crows in Winter

Some crows sat blabbing atop a roof
to see the world from an upscale view
with heads pulled in and feathers fluffed
they braved the biting winter dusk

And watched and listened, cawed sometimes
the colder it grew, the darker the sky.
A chimney emerged from a roof ridge nearby
emitting smoke from a cozy fire.

And softly the snow began drifting down,
so wispy at first, then fluffy as down
and as it was snowing, said crow number one,
"time to get going, my friend, lets run."

"No, stupid," said crow number two, "we'll stay.
that chimney up there is the perfect place
to warm us in comfort." And eager he leapt
to settle himself at the chimney's edge.

Urged crow number one, "let's go right now,
'ere the snow piles high and keeps us down."
"We're staying put," said crow number two,
"we'll not catch cold nor even the flu."

Crows and other Pedestrians

Felicitous crow number one gave in,
moved close to the inner chimney rim.
"A better crow am I," said he
then pushed forth his chest to catch the heat.

The crows huddled close at the inner rim
the snow had no power, the warmth made them grin
they leant their bodies to the rising warmth –
daybreak discovered two cured and smoked forms.

There's a Nazi in my Closet

Throwing away things is for some people a very difficult thing to do. Consider the following scenario: there is leftover food in the refrigerator. You know that nobody will eat it voluntarily, and you don't have the time or energy to deal with it. Sure, you promised yourself: tonight's the night. But when you get home, tired from a day of work at the office, you're being bombarded with the latest school gossip from one of your children while the other one, overwhelmed by the prattle power of the sibling, is reduced to anxious and silent waiting for equal time. Add to that the conflict between a programmed need for cooking a meal versus trying to avoid it because the kids hate your cooking, all the while your easy chair is calling you from the TV room...

If the leftovers were a suitably large amount of, let's say, a casserole dish that would be enough for all and easy to reheat, it wouldn't be so bad. But no, it's a little bit of something that doesn't go with anything else, stored in a microwave dish that can't go on the stove, and the microwave is on the blink. So you don't warm up the leftovers again, and you know deep down inside that you never will, but years of childhood indoctrination about the sinfulness of throwing away food while half the world goes to bed hungry prevents you from dumping it. A few days later you have a good excuse - it's rotten now.

One of my children is a packrat who not only hangs on to every carton and box that ever came with a present, but she also collects outgrown sweaters, and knick-knacks, snippets of shiny cloth, bits of yarn, patches of lace, every picture she ever drew, stuffed animals and all sorts of odds and ends, and if I didn't take occasional pity on her inability to part with anything, her collections would induce permanent disorientation.

That's not as bad as what I was faced with from an uncle of mine. Over the years he had collected all sorts of objects that had great sentimental value for him but nothing else, and because he wanted neither to part with them nor keep them he decided to bless me with his prizes. For posterity, he said, cleverly having waited for a moment when I was out of my head with a severe case of the flu. Among the "treasures" were antique audio tapes, German beer coasters he had collected during his army time, jars and bottles of uncommon shape or color, old lanterns, picture frames and rusty tin objects of indefinable usage.

All this stuff wandered into my basement where it collected dust, webs, and mold. When my posterity moved out, the junk remained. I ended up feeling guilty for getting rid of that which my uncle treasured. Only resentment for his audacity and my gullibility finally ended the guilt.

A history professor I came to know and appreciate, who had graciously given me access to his library of recent European history, told me over the phone one day that he wanted to give me a picture that was very dear to him and would I be willing to accept it. I said that I would. Then he told me - and he hemmed and hawed about it and obviously had trouble wording it, and he admitted that he hoped he wouldn't make a wrong impression - he told me that the picture, a very nice one and beautifully framed, was a portrait of Hitler. His rather timid revelation made me laugh, but I stuck to my word that I would accept it.

Later, though, I had second thoughts. The realization that Hitler's psychopathic energies might affect my peaceful home life worried me. Then I thought that I could always keep the frame and throw away the picture. It made me feel guilty. Perhaps I would tell him that I had changed my mind.

When I got to his house with my husband in tow, he explained to us that although he was born in the USA, his French-born mother had taken him to France where he grew up during the German occupation. The portrait of Hitler had been given to him as a prize during his high school years. We liked the Germans very much, he said to me who is a native German.

After that comment I didn't have the heart to tell him that I didn't want it. He went and brought the picture. It was as he said, quite nice really. The photographer must have caught Hitler during one of his better moments; he is standing by a window, slightly bent forward and looking out and down at something or someone, with a rather benevolent smile on his face. I accepted the picture. He made me promise to take good care of it. His children, unfortunately, couldn't care less about history, he explained.

Now I'm stuck with a portrait of Hitler. I think I'll stuff it in my closet. Some people have skeletons in their closets; I guess I'll have a Nazi in mine.

Mother's Happy Day

Celebrating Christmas in Germany of the 1950s included for my family a visit to the cemetery. "Who will walk, and who will ride?" Father would ask during the early afternoon of Christmas Eve. We already knew the answer; the little kids would ride with Father and Mother, and the big kids would walk because the car was too small for nine children and two adults. It was a baby blue Volkswagen Beetle, which Father persisted in driving to spite his extravagant brother and business partner, Karl, who had no children at all but drove a Mercedes.

The VW served us well enough; one child on Mother's lap in the passenger seat, three children on the back seat with two more on their laps, and two of the smaller ones stuffed sideways, with knees drawn up tightly to their chests, in the space behind the back seat. That left only one for walking.

But no one ever walked alone to the cemetery on Christmas Eve. Visiting the silent, agreeable members of the family among the stalwart chrysanthemums at the base of a tall, prominent gravestone was just the somber prelude to the giddy fun of opening presents. Arm-in-arm, in a steady rhythmic gait of almost musical quality, two or three of us older girls walked through streets that were deserted by pedestrians and most cars. Stores had closed at noon. Young and Old were at home preparing for the holiday. A fine mist enveloped houses, streets, and us in a thin shroud of mystery that fired the imagination with tingling anticipation.

Like the rest of the city, the cemetery lay silent and utterly deserted. On the gravestone that dominated the family plot were engraved the names of Father's parents, his brother Ernst who had died at age fifteen, and Father's handsome brother John who was killed during World War I and lay buried somewhere in France. Father's maiden aunt rested nearby, and in the children's section lay his baby brother and sister.

Mother had set up the grave lantern on All Saints Day, November 1. It stood almost three feet tall on three legs in the middle of the large plot. Its candle had long since burned down and Mother replaced it with a new one and lit it with a match. She picked some dead leaves off the spruce branches that covered the bare soil, and talked about replanting with begonias in the spring. We said prayers for everyone. Father became nostalgic then.

From trees and shrubs the mist ran off in steady droplets and soaked the ground. It didn't take long for the damp cold to creep into our stocking-clad legs. It sent us home at a fast pace.

It was getting dark then, and colder. Town houses along the way stood introspective, silent and dark in the eerie stillness of the lead gray twilight. Through gaps in drawn window curtains we glimpsed festive white candle lights on Christmas trees of highly intimate celebrations.

On Christmas Eve, we knew, Mother would be fun. She would not vent on us her frustration and anger, would not be harsh and cross with us. There would be no abusive reprimands or unjust punishment to make us hate her. She would not give the broomstick a work-out on our bare legs and then demand that we suffer the pain silently or get more of the same. Today and tomorrow, Mother would not have to think about working in the family store and, perhaps, her feet would not hurt so much. There would be no thinking of Father's meddling sisters who considered themselves a step above Mother on the social ladder. There would be no talk about the torment that Mother had suffered at the hands of her in-laws for being just a dumb country bumpkin who, nonetheless, turned out to have better business sense than they; for locking them out of her life in an act of self-preservation; for taking control over Father away from them; for growing a garden and making profit in the store; for giving birth to nine healthy children while they, Father's three surviving siblings, had produced exactly one between them. Christmas would bring out in Mother a rare sense of humor, would make her laugh easily and sing blissfully off-key, and it would make her forget family feud and isolation.

After returning from the cemetery, Father and Mother had company in the living room while we children were kept waiting in the playroom. Mother kept us waiting, and excitement turned into agitation, and tension built up to an unbearable pitch until it exploded in anger and frustration in the younger children while we older ones, straining to keep our own composure, were unable to calm them. Mother poked her head through the door now and then to tell us that the wait was almost over. She had company so rarely, and the smile on her face was so blissful that we didn't dare complain. So we waited.

When company left, Mother and Father did some last minute flitting about in and out of the formal dining room and through it to the piano room where the nativity had been set up. We hadn't been allowed to watch, but we had known from the appearance in our apartment upstairs of a certain employee from Father's business downstairs that something was underway. The secrecy of it all had been nearly as exciting as the great event.

Every year, the nativity layout was made larger until it had reached the size of a bed, had three large plaster cliffs and a rock cave for the Holy Family. A most realistic touch had been achieved with the help of a laundry basket full of moss and other greens we had collected during a Sunday outing with the Nativity Club.

Opposite the nativity stood the glossy black piano that Father had once rescued from the rubble of a neighbor's bombed house. Between nativity and piano stood the

Christmas tree, a seven foot spruce, emaciated looking in its natural state with branches too far apart, but with ornaments hung and fine heavy tinsel reflecting a thousand fold the flames of carefully placed real candles, the tree was a glorious sight to behold.

The dining room and the piano room were kept locked until Christmas Eve, and when it was time, Mother came for us with her blissful smile. She and Father led us to the piano room to sing Christmas carols, accompanied by one or the other of us older children on the piano, and recite poetry by the nativity. We ogled the slightly open door that led to the dining room in hopes of getting a glimpse of the presents, we knew were spread out there on table, chairs, and sideboard, for each one of us our own little pile. We didn't know which pile belonged to whom until Mother took us by the hand and led us to it.

Father became frisky then. He sang the song about the Christmas tree with many lights, but he changed the words and sang about a prune that his dumb brother had hung on the tree. We knew he was singing about his brother with whom Father managed the family business but could never get along. The words rhymed so well that it made us laugh, and Mother scolded with mock indignation, "husband, stop that!"

This was Mother's Happy Day. The spirit of Christmas gave Mother, who could never share herself and who, through two devastating wars had become frugal to a fault, license to give to her heart's content. On that one day of the year, tradition gave her permission to spoil us with impunity, to give in to our wishes and wants without fear of fostering willfulness, to make up for injustices because she could not apologize, to beg forgiveness without losing face.

A Homecoming

Spirits were as high in the United States as they were in Germany when the Berlin Wall came tumbling down. After decades of political and social actions on all levels had failed to re-unite Germany, the bloodless, almost effortless event of November 1989 seemed to poke fun at the powers that were. For me, who had left Germany in 1961 to marry an American GI, the event culminated in a long overdue, most wonderful kind of home-coming.

I grew up in the 1950s when nationalist sentiments were not in vogue in post-war Germany. My business school education included very few social studies and humanities. An immature love of Spitzweg's paintings and Mozart's music, instilled by a wise old teacher, was not nurtured enough to blossom into an individual search for cultural roots and connectedness. The adults in my life, not knowing the importance of having a national identity, promoted and fostered a religious identity instead. I rummaged through my Father's history books but didn't understand them. Questions and answers were not fostered because providing for nine children demanded too much time and energy. No one talked to us about the past. No one attempted to nurture in us a sense of responsibility for cultural heritage and historical truth.

A vacuum existed and it was filled by the dominant presence of the American military. We loved American chocolate and candies and especially that curious thing called chewing gum. If chewed in the proper way, with lots of tongue action kneading and rolling the gum around in a wide-open mouth cavity, it bestowed an image of sophistication on the chewer – or so we thought. My father forbade this cud-chewing habit with the same passion with which he forbade everything he perceived to be coming from the United States.

But the vacuum pulled and tugged. There was the fascinating sound of the American speech. It seemed to emanate from words being lolled around the mouth cavity, much like chewing gum, before being expelled from a deep hollow in the back of the mouth. The endless military convoys exuded a sense of power that lured us to our third floor windows. We liked the friendly GIs who were enchanted by blond children and stroked their curly heads and cried with delight "hi, blonde."

With the deepening of the Cold War came a deepening of American commitment in Germany. Social doors at the army base, called Downs Barracks, began to open in an attempt to foster German-American friendship. Parties and teenagers, make-up and cocktails, cornflakes and beef stake began to infiltrate our language and household. At the army base, German girls could meet GIs who beguiled with casual behavior, small pay but much German money, and a worldly sophistication that was engendered by the uniform. As victors in a foreign country, without the child-classification that the presence of a set of parents would bestow, they had an aura of importance, of being a United States representative.

And there was more; lots of Wild West movies. They were played to the exclusion of any other genre in the movie theater in our large downtown building. Tom Mix, Hop-along Cassidy and Kid Carson were the subjects of my first American history lessons. Errol Flynn and John Wayne were the first movie stars I knew by name. Since we owned the house, we saw the movies for free. Not that Mother allowed such a frivolous waste of time. There was too much work to be done in a household of eleven people, not to mention the retail store on the first floor, and the huge vegetable garden my Mother took pride in. But children are so inventive. In that corner of our courtyard where townhouse and warehouse meet was the side entrance to the movie theater. A spiral staircase lead from there to the projection room above. On this staircase we could sit and look through the slats of a ventilator and watch the film. Unfortunately, this heavenly spot was visible from our kitchen window, and it happened from time to time that the viewer on the forbidden spot, lost in the exotic adventure, was brought back most effectively by a bucket full of cold water, shot at him from the kitchen window. It was better during summer weekends when the exit doors of the theater were left open. We could then hide in the heavy curtains at the exit and not only watch but also hear the movie. In a house full of children, it was possible to take off for a little while without Mother noticing right away, and with a bit of luck we could see quite a chunk of the movie. But it was most distressing when the movie made us forget everything else including the time until Mother's loud, sharp call from the kitchen window, shocked us back to reality, which affected the unsuspecting soul as dramatically as cold water did the warm body.

At age eighteen, nineteen the privacy of the courtyard became more important than the movies. Mother had a thing about boyfriends - they were not allowed. Being with a young man had to be done on the sneak, and the quiet darkness of the courtyard was the only place of privacy available to us girls. But Mother must have remembered her own sneaky ways because occasionally the romantic interlude came to an abrupt end when Mother's loud, sharp call from the kitchen window, easily heard even inside the movie house, turned serenity into anxiety.

With an army base in my hometown, known to the American military as Downs Barracks, and a major maneuver site known as Wildflecken about twenty miles away, it was inevitable that I should meet a GI. When Father fist knew about it he had a fit. Being American was a strike against him. Father had him investigated and discovered that his civilian profession was neither prestigious nor financially rewarding. Two strikes against him. To make matters worse, my GI was not Catholic. Three strikes and he was out - unseen and unheard.

When I reached legal age at twenty-one my parents could no longer hold me. I went to the U.S. and married my GI. For fifteen years of isolation from friends and family I served him faithfully, tried to do and be American in every way because he preferred it. But it never really worked. In the end, being neither German nor American, I was nothing. This condition led to illness. Illness led to insight, and insight led to divorce.

Later, I married an African whose ancient nation had long held in high esteem German culture, intelligence and discipline. My husband's high esteem for the German people in general transferred to me in particular, and now I began to grow and thrive in every way very rapidly, and a national consciousness developed quite spontaneously.

And then one day, shortly after the Berlin wall came tumbling down, I heard the German national anthem played on the radio. I heard it as though for the very first time – solemn and serene, full of fervor, and despite the joyful words with a touch of sadness. An unspeakably warm sensation suddenly came over me and tears welled up in my eyes, and for the first time in my fifty-year life I knew where I belonged.

Nis Randers by Otto Ernst

translated by Rita Traut Kabeto

Nis was a Frisian, a member of a Germanic tribe that lived
along the Northern coast of Holland, roughly between the
rivers Rhein in the West and Ems in the East. They had
their own culture and language, but not much of it is left
now.

Crashing and howling and bursting night
darkness aflame with furious might
a cry through the breakers.

The sky is on fire and it's clear as day
on the sandbank a shipwreck, still rocked by the waves
but gyres are pulling.

Nis Randers has seen, and calmly he says,
"one man is left clinging, out there, on the mast
we'll get him, we must."

And gripping his arm, his mother says, "no!
you're all I have left, I can't let you go
I will it, your mother.

"Your father was drowned and Momme, my son,
and Uwe is missing these three years past
my Uwe, your brother."

With foot on the bridge, his mother in back
he points to the wreck, and calmly he says,
"and his mother?"

Boat up and boat down, what a hellish dance
it's bursting to pieces, no, not yet.
how long will it hold?

With fiery whips the ocean does lash
the man-eating horses, this way and that,
they're foaming and raging.

Their panting speed has coupled them tight
they rear and crowd each other with might
with hooves that are thrashing.

Three storms at once! They torch the world
wat's that? A boat! It's headed for shore
they made it. They're coming!

And eyes and ears are straining to know.
Quiet! A call! And then once more,
"tell Mother, it's Uwe!"

All You Ever Wanted to Know
about refugee resettlement - but never thought to ask

My husband is a voluntary one-man refugee-resettlement program. Not that he had intended it that way; he simply got stuck with the job when the other volunteers disappeared. It all started when he and his group of countrymen were asked to sponsor some refugees from their native country, Ethiopia. First came two families with small children, then a young couple with an adolescent relative, then followed three single young men, then I lost count. Each new arrival was preceded by frantic running around in search of funding, housing, cheap household furnishings, and after arrival trips to the airport, the immigration office, the social security office, the welfare office, the refugee clinic, the refugee center, and a ride on the city bus system to learn that. Telephone service, electric service, gas service, bus passes, and personal IDs had to be gotten. And just when everyone had settled down very nicely a new batch of refugees arrived and it started all over again.

Then people needed medical care for colds, flu, goiters, syphilis, malaria, stomach and intestinal problems, involving countless trips to clinics, doctors, specialists, hospitals. One depressed young woman who had run the gamut of medical providers, including psychiatry, finally revealed that she and her husband had married in Sudan while waiting for exit visas solely for the purpose of speeding up proceedings for the partner who was way down on the waiting list. After arrival in the US the couple was to split up and go their separate ways. But the husband had changed his mind and his wife felt pressured. Another young woman in the same predicament fared much worse; her husband beat her up, and my husband's mediating efforts, sometimes in the middle of the night, were rewarded with accusations of being the cause of the problem.

There is a husband who had promised his wife on his sick bed that he would stop smoking, and when she caught him sneaking a cigarette she demanded a divorce.

Meanwhile, most everybody had found a job or two and worked long hours to make it. Since none of them had established credit ratings the banks would neither cash their paychecks nor open accounts for them, and my husband went looking for other options for cashing checks, and he became temporary savings bank for some of them. But working 10-16 hours per day left no time for learning English. The initial government sponsored lessons were almost useless, and without sufficient English skills they continue to need my husband's help with interpretations, mediations, and counseling.

Then some of the fellows were able to buy cars, so my husband helped with the purchase, gave driving lessons, bought insurance, and interpreted the driving tests. The motor vehicle department took it for granted that the interpreter translated correct answers from the applicant rather than fixing wrong answers in the translation. In April, we struggled not only with our own tax return but several others as well. Meanwhile, someone had lost his wallet with all IDs, and the round of the agencies was on again.

A local church group had graciously donated the use of a very large house just in time for the arrival of a family of ten from Angola. Several other single people and small families could temporarily be housed there, including a young woman with a hyperactive child. Pretty soon the child's behavior began to disturb the others; a single man didn't want to abide by the curfew rule; another young man brought female visitors; a young woman had seizures; the size of the heating bill became outrageous; the carpets were soiled; and the church finally asked everyone except the Angolan family to leave. My husband found affordable housing for the young woman with seizures, just before he realized that she could not possibly live by herself. A call to the epileptic foundation seemed promising, but the diagnosis turned out negative for epilepsy. Now what!

Thanks to my husband's counseling efforts the couple that had fought over smoking was reconciled while the other young couple broke up according to the original plan, and the woman left town without so much as a day's notice to her employer who had given her work on my husband's recommendations. And when the abusive husband was persuaded to leave his wife, the welfare office had to be persuaded to give her a share of support. Meanwhile, two young families who first had shared one apartment wanted to split up, and the housing search was on again.

There is a refugee who had married a woman in Sudan after he had applied for an immigration visa. The authorities refused to recognize her as his spouse and she was not permitted to come with him. A frantic correspondence ensued between husband, wife, and immigration, all to be translated and notarized. Another young man wants to send money to his wife back home. He goes about it so carefully for fear of loss or theft that it never gets there at all, which necessitates several trips to the bank to get the money back.

Then my husband was asked to sponsor eight single young Libyan men who had, with the support, approval, and instigation of the United States government, trained in Chad for the removal of Qaddafi but had failed, could no longer live in Libya now and were brought by the state department to the US for resettlement. Thank God, my husband doesn't speak Arabic.

Sprechen Sie Deutsch?

Sprache – Mittel zum Zweck der Verwirrung.

Neulich sagte meine Schwester ich sei komisch. Das ist weiter nichts Neues; sie hat es vor Jahren auch schon gesagt. Obgleich ich damals noch nicht so geistreich war wie heute so wusste ich doch sogleich was sie damit meinte.

Heute bin ich mir nicht mehr so sicher. Meint sie vielleicht dass ich komisch bin wie eine Oper komisch ist? Wohl nicht. Vielleicht bin ich eigenartig. Aber ich kann ja nur meine eigene Art besitzen und nicht eine andere Art. Wenn ich eine andere Art besitzen wuerde, dann waere ich andersartig, nicht eigenartig. Vielleicht meint meine Schwester ich bin sonderbar. Unter diesem Wort verweist mich das Woerterbuch zu eigenartig. Da gibt es noch wunderlich. Aber das kann auch nicht auf mich bezogen sein, denn was habe ich mit Wundern zu tun. Healt mich meine Schwester fuer merkwuerdig? Des Merkens wuerdig bin ich ganz sicher, aber der Ton ihrer Stimme drueckte etwas Anderes aus. Vielleicht meint sie seltsam. Das Woerterbuch erklaert es folgendermassen: vom Ueblichen abweichend und nicht recht begreiflich. Ich glaube nicht, dass meine Schwester mich unbegreiflich findet. Ihre Ausdrucksweise laesst mit Sicherheit auf groesste innerste Ueberzeugung schliessen.

So viele Moeglichkeiten des muendlichen Ausdrucks gibt es und ich weiss trotzdem nicht wie meine Schwester ueber mich denkt. Die Sprache ist schon eine komische Sache. Komisch! Aha! Jetzt weiss ich's wieder.

Crows in Summer

Some crow birds clung to a longish wire,
a heavily thick one for telephonire
crow number one was picking so deft
on a bone in his claw, acquired by theft.

He picked at the bone so heartily
that crow number two felt jealousy
and loudly demanded, "you selfish one, you
save some for me, I am hungry too."

But crow number one turned his back on her
and continued to pick, could not be deterred
and mumbled with beak full of food half chewed
"there's not enough meat on this bone for two."

Crows and other Pedestrians

Crow number two did scold and whine
In vain she was seeking a friendly invite
But all of a sudden the bone did drop
To the sidewalk below with a loudish plop.

Crow number one then anxiously flew
down to the sidewalk his bone to rescue.
He failed to notice a car shooting forth
from the neighboring house's garage door

The crow was careless, saw only the bone
the driver saw neither, ran over them both.
But crow number two hurried down real quick
delighted herself with a crow picnic.

Great Expectations

Well, I did it again! I don't know how it happens, but while I was busy with Christmas preparations, Christmas came and went and passed me by again. I planned so hard and long for it to be perfect.

I firmly believe in an Advent season - a time for inner preparations and happy anticipation with advent wreaths and advent calendars, and yearning advent music and secret shopping and gift making and cookie baking.

During my childhood in post-war Germany, neither children nor adults were asked what they wanted. There was no need for it; since you knew the person you had a pretty good idea what would please him or her. The post-war years were not affluent, and even a practical gift to fill a need was appreciated.

As a result, and because presents were kept hidden till Christmas Eve, children never got the notion that they had a right to receive presents. For children, gifts were dependent on good behavior, and since children misbehave at times they could never be sure if they would get anything. The resultant mystery added spice to what might otherwise have been a boringly pious Advent observance.

I try to reproduce this air of excitement and mystery within my own family, so I ignore weeks of television news analysis of the American Christmas story - you know the one: will they buy or won't they buy. I close my eyes and ears to the constant stream of Christmas music and Christmas decorations and Christmas gifts and Christmas TV programs, and I never, no never, take my children into the hub of the great American pastime - the shopping mall.

After the subdued mood of the Advent season, Christmas would come as a great joyous event rather abruptly bursting in upon us with the performance of the first Christmas ritual. There would be preparations, of course, baking a large quantity of cookies, perhaps seven or eight varieties, and enough to last the entire season. The Christmas mail must be posted to arrive in time for Christmas. The children's best clothes must be laundered and ironed. The house should be clean from top to bottom and nicely decorated. The Christmas tree must not go up too soon, and as a last touch, the silver must be polished and the nativity set up on the 23rd of December.

Then, on Christmas Eve, we would first go to children's evening mass to celebrate the spiritual aspect of the holiday. We adults would glow with the excitement of recaptured memories of many happy Christmases. After mass, we would come home and play some Christmas music on the piano, sing carols together by the tree, maybe recite a poem or two. And then would come the giddy fun part of opening presents.

But the modern way of life does not lend itself to the execution of such romantic notions. High Taxes, high interest rates, and low incomes force both parents to work, and a high unemployment rate necessitates an attitude of job first. How much time or leisure can there be left over for anything else! I didn't get the house cleaned or decorated or the silver polished. I also did not get more than the most important Christmas mail sent out. I baked only two varieties of cookies at the last minute and not in delicious secrecy. My son's jacket was less than impeccable and he had to wear his worn shoes because there was no money to buy him new ones. My daughter had forgotten her warm coat in her school locker and was shivering in her thin little jacket.

While mass might have lifted my spirit to the proper heights the worry over her fairly bad cold getting worse on the frigid walk home very definitely kept it down. Then, it suddenly hit me that I had forgotten to set up the nativity, and now my spirit not only didn't get off the ground, it plummeted.

I still had hopes for Christmas day. My older children with their little ones were to come around ten in the morning but they did not show up till noon. Their kids were feverish, my daughter was sick, her husband not much better. All the presents were opened all at once while I was busy catching the Christmas spirit on film, so I never learned what each person received from whom. The big kids and their families left soon afterward to visit in-laws. They meant to come back for dinner, but too much ice on the roads kept them away.

Now my house is quiet again. The presents are put away, the wrappings saved for next year, and all that's left is the Christmas tree. It's the first thing I turn on in the morning and the last thing I turn off at night. Shiny ornaments and gently swaying tinsel reflect the tree's little white lights thousand fold. In the darkened room, and looking without my eyeglasses, the tree is a sky full of delicately flickering stars. There it stands, a thing of beauty, demanding nothing, disturbing no one. I can hardly tear myself away from this magnificent vision that was neither anticipated nor planned for but discovered quite by chance.

Riddle

A man dies and goes to hell. He finds that there are different hells for different countries. He goes to the German hell and asks, "what do they do here?"

He is told that, "first they put you in an electric chair for an hour. Then they lay you on a bed of nails for another hour. Then the German devil comes in and bites you for the rest of the day."

The man does not like the sound of this so he moves on. He checks out the USA hell as well as the Russian hell and many more. He discovers that all are similar to the German hell.

Then he comes to the Ethiopian hell and finds that there is a long line of people waiting to get in. Amazed, he asks, "what do they do here?"

He was told, "first they put you in an electric chair for an hour, then they lay you on a bed of nails for another hour. Then the Ethiopian devil comes and bites you for the rest of the day."

"But that is exactly the same as all the other hells. Why are so many people waiting to get in here?"

"Because there is never any electricity so the electric chair doesn't work; and the nails were paid for but were never delivered by the contractor so the bed is comfortable; and the Ethiopian devil used to be a civil servant; he comes in, signs his time sheet and goes back home to other business."

Anonymous

Weekends are for Fun?

Tomorrow is Monday, and when I get to the office my co-workers are going to ask how my weekend was. They always do that. I suspect they want to be asked in return so that they can tell about all the great fun they had. I always say, "fine." What else am I going to say? That I searched the want ads for a better job? That I spent hours unplugging my plugged-up toilet because my youngest child thought its teddy bear needed a bath? That I shopped for groceries, did laundry? I should think that all people who work full time do these very same things on their weekends. But people talk about the fun they had, especially if the sun had been shining which, it seems, is conducive to having fun.

I don't know what the fuss is all about. Come to think of it, I don't really know what they mean with the word fun. I come from a very serious minded family. We had birthday and wedding celebrations, and special events usually connected with religious observations, but fun?

My American College Dictionary describes it as "mirthful (joyous, jolly, gay, amused) sport or diversion, merry amusement, joking playfulness." Hmm. I don't think any of these adjectives apply to my weekends - merry laundry? Mirthful yard work? jolly toilet unstuffing? I don't get it.

I found a clue in the Friday newspaper, which is full of ads about fun that can be had on the weekend, and all that fun usually includes food, or drink, or both. Maybe if I snack on some goodies while I unplug the toilet, scrub the floors, do laundry...naaah. It doesn't look like sport or diversion, merry amusement or joking playfulness can be achieved by doing housework drudgery.

TV ads often depict fun as easy and simple and very spontaneous, but almost always reserved for sexually active young people. When older people are shown to have fun it's due to the rewards of using certain products designed for the achievement of good bowel habits and bladder control.

While I wasn't vigilant enough, my children became infected with this fun-seeking virus. Every Friday after school they start asking me what we are going to do on the weekends. Needless to say, they don't want to know about the chores I have lined up for them; they're thinking of "fun" things to do, and their kind of fun, so they seem to think, can only be found outside the home and only in connection with spending money. Since my income is small and I can't afford to take them anywhere it would seem logical to conclude that my children rarely have any fun. But wait! Almost every day at school, my daughter spies another oh, so fine a guy, and that makes her ever so gay. And my son's playful way of teasing his little brother causes the latter much mirth. And what about all that merry amusement when their father, with his heavy foreign accent, turns regular English into comedy! When my daughter gets to spend the night with a friend or goes shopping for clothes without my supervision she is all of merry and gay and jolly. The same is true for my son when he gets to spend the day with his best friend, when I give up a TV show to read to him, or when pussycat lavishes her catty affections on him. Now, if they are merry and amused and jolly and gay, then they must be having fun.

If having a good time is the same as having fun, then yes, I do have fun. After thirty years of mothering - just being home alone, no one to do for, finally being able to do my own thing in my own way, undisturbed and uninterrupted. That is great fun.

Retirement will be a blast!

All You Need is a Great Resume

Really?

That's what Mother thought - Mother who never had to look for work. The terms underqualified, overqualified, underemployed were totally foreign to her. Actually, I suspect that these terms were invented for the purpose of refusing an applicant without saying so. A classic covert action designed to confuse him so that he won't notice that his rights have been violated. Mother had it easy - with Father's family business and nine children she had plenty of work and never needed a resume.

Nowadays, looking for work is a complicated thing. It ought to be easy enough when one has only a high school diploma; every employer requires it, and making up a resume should be a breeze. Once you have a college degree, though, writing a resume becomes more complex because now you need to show that your work experience was gained in your field of study. Anything else, forget it. Of course if you list no work experience you will seem like a lazy bum. That certainly won't endear you to a prospective employer. Even when you do have experience in your field of study or a related field, the chances that you have exactly the required combination of knowledge, skills, performance level, and experience are extremely slim. Sometimes, a prospective employer will count experience for a lacking degree. But how you would get that experience without the degree, is anybody's guess.

You have heard it said that the more education you have the better off you are? Don't you believe it. With two or more degrees you are in for a hardship. Your area of job search is much broader now, and the possible combinations of education and work experience are endless. You do realize that you cannot simply list all your education and all work experience in one resume. It would never work. Since you don't want a prospective employer in, let's say the academic field, to know that you have done simple labor, for fear of creating a negative impression, then your resume must not reflect that work. This will create a gap in work history, and you'll be suspect of being either lazy or unmotivated. And vise versa: should you try for a service job because you have to eat while you're trying to get into a career, your resume must not reflect your advanced degree because your prospective employer will assume, and rightfully so, that you will leave as soon as you find something better. So you don't mention your advanced degree, but now you can also not mention any related work, and the experience section of your resume will be sparse, and there go your chances down the drain again.

You pretty much have to create a new resume for every job application, and after you have done this a few dozen times the mere mention of resume will move you to tears.

Then there is the cover letter. You're supposed to say why you want this job. I need to eat. Sorry, that won't cut it. You try to play up your special assets: you're bilingual. Sorry, they need Russian and Japanese. You tell them you're a fast learner, willing to work overtime to pick up what you might be lacking. Dead silence. Actually, such eagerness can be counted against you; makes you look desperate. Nobody wants a desperate employee.

Trying to straighten out a prospective employer on the idea that just because you have accidentally landed in a particular field doesn't mean that it was your life's goal is a futile effort. And don't ever say that you need benefits, or more income, or a job closer to home because you no longer own a car. The resulting silence will make you think the world has gone away.

You might tell them that you love to serve, that you're even willing and able to brew a good cup of coffee. Now you know, and I know, that most every office would go for that. But no. Makes you sound too housewify. That's not career material. I suspect that words such as serve – and there is a similar one: obedience – awakens visions of cloisters and submissiveness, even servitude. Makes today's sophisticated business world awfully uncomfortable. That's not to say that the employer doesn't want submissiveness to the existing order, but he cannot say that for fear of attracting sheep, and that would hurt his image. What he wants are thinkers who don't think on company time. Then he wonders why his carefully laid plans for employee retention don't work.

Never call yourself a Jack-of-all-traits to show your versatility. That's a bad word. You cannot be a career oriented individual if you jump from job to job, never mind that your life's circumstances have forced you into frequent job changes.

What today's employers want are people who fit into nonagonal niches. You're flexible, you tell them; you'll squeeze in, you assure them. But such promises are suspect in an environment where extra effort is dictated, not volunteered.

Just when you think you have reached your frustration threshold you come across an application form in which a company wants to convince you that it carefully guards all your civil rights. So, please fill in your name, race and sex. This information is only intended for federal and state statistical purposes, and you are not obligated to comply. What kind of statistical data can be gleaned when filling out the forms is done arbitrarily? Invalid data, I should think. Then why do the Fed and State spend my money on the collection of invalid data? Maybe it's really the employer who wants to know. Covert action at work again.

But, you go along because you still trust that your rights are being guarded by the benevolent power of the State. After all, the constitution guarantees the promotion of general welfare and insures domestic tranquility. And there can be neither welfare nor tranquility when one' right are being stomped upon. Then you discover the last page of this application form where it says that "employment and compensation can be terminated at any time with or without cause and with or without notice, at the option of the company..." And after the initial shock has worn off and frustration has given way to cynicism you marvel at the perversion of constitutional intent which forces us not only to tolerate but even knowingly consent to the abuse and corruption of our rights.   1992

The Enemy Within

State and federal income statistics maintain that I'm a poor person, under-privileged, socio-economically deprived, poverty-stricken even. I don't know about that. I don't feel any different from the time when I earned twice as much as I do now. It's a rather new experience for me, so perhaps I don't understand yet what it means to be under-privileged. My AMERICAN COLLEGE DICTIONARY defines it as, "denied the enjoyment of the normal privileges or rights of a society because of low economic and social status."

Hmm. Low economic status. I can identify with that. But notice that the definition says "low economic and social status," not "economic or social status." In other words, economic and social statuses go hand-in-hand. It means that if my income is low then my social status is automatically also low. I would call that prejudice: "an unfavorable opinion or feeling formed beforehand or without knowledge, thought, or reason." It appears that our social stratification is arranged not on such merits as wisdom, or intellect, or creativity, but on the amount of money entrepreneurial elements see fit to pay for a given type of work, regardless of social or cultural value.

The first part of the definition says, "Denied the enjoyment of the normal privileges or rights." What rights? What privileges? I can still vote. I can still sit in judgment over others as a juror. My kids still get educated, and the libraries are still open to me. I can enjoy golden sunshine and silvery moon beams, ancient trees, charming people and fragrant flowers, awe-inspiring music and art. My apple trees will grow another crop of apples, and my grape vine will produce grapes again. I can still pick wild blackberries in August and eat delicious pies all winter. I can watch opera on public TV even without paying and I can complain to anyone about anything. My long-time friends have not deserted me and my family is always with me. What am I missing?

Granted, I can't go shopping in prestigious stores, but then I never believed in wasting my money in the support of the excessively affluent life styles of corporate bosses anyway. I had to sell my second car when I couldn't afford to repair it, but I'm saving on gas, insurance, and licensing, and I walk a lot more - my favorite exercise. My kids can't go to see the latest movies, but waiting for them to come to TV is no hardship. Besides, I'll censor them anyway. We don't go out much, but we don't miss that because we are actively involved in a number of people adventures. What's more, we enjoy being at home because we don't need to loose ourselves in a crowd. I don't eat steak because I prefer vegetarian food. My kids become inventive with few toys, willing to strive for good grades to get scholarships, modest in their expectations, and grateful for little things. My mind is free from investment worries, yet I suffer no anxiety about my future because I know it is safe in the hands of a higher power. What am I missing?

All right, underprivileged I'm not. How about socio-economically deprived. That sounds like a more stilted version of the same condition. Then there is poverty-stricken. Stricken with poverty the way a person is stricken with cancer? When one is stricken with cancer one gets very upset, to say the least. There lurks the threat of untimely death, not to speak of the physical hardship of chemotherapy and radiation therapy. Family members get very worried, of course, and anxious, even depressed. - I don't think I'm stricken.

I am also being classified as poor. My dictionary describes it as "having little or nothing in the way of wealth, goods, or means of subsistence. Dependent upon charity." Dependent upon charity I am, but I loose no sleep over it. For one thing, I have contributed for years to that fund from which I now draw. What's more, our society with its high taxes, high interest rates, and high prices insists on being greedy on the one hand while it underpays me for my services on the other hand. I cannot be held accountable for the discrepancy. After all, if the amount of one's wage is not set to meet the financial demands of one's society, to enable individuals to support themselves adequately, then what is the determining factor? If we don't care about people who or what do we care about? Where is the brotherhood we sing about in the national anthem? While we should be striving to bring about the brotherhood of peoples we ask God to bestow it upon us instead. Very clever: when it doesn't materialize we can claim that He did not will it.

Do I wish for more money? Of course I do. I also wish for a secure job with plenty of benefits. It's a constant struggle and there is much denial in order to make ends meet. But life is a struggle, and who is to say that my struggle is any better or worse than anybody else's. And while I am struggling with my lot I am still free to enjoy all the beauty that surrounds me. —

But then, a black cloud moved in and hovered over my life. The dentist said so himself as he attempted a simple repair job, which revealed the need for a root-canal, which revealed the need for an extraction, which led to the loss of a crown, which added up to well over two thousand dollars' worth of needed repairs. Even if I had insurance I still wouldn't be able to handle the deductible. Now what do I do! I can't walk around with gaps in my teeth. I won't have front-office appearance. I'll lose what little employment I have left.

Then my grown son was diagnosed with cancer. He fought it successfully, but he'll never qualify for individual health insurance coverage again. Then I began to worry about my daughter and her husband and children who also have no health insurance. Every penny I manage to put aside for my younger children's college education, future car or appliance repairs, perhaps even a rare vacation - so I think in moments of giddy optimism - is eaten up by medical bills, and the debts only grow. With every windstorm I fear that my rickety chimney will come crashing down, that my rotting front porch will cause someone an accident, that the brown water from my bathroom faucet is a sign of rusting pipes, that my mother will die and I won't have the money to be at her funeral to fulfill my last duty to her.

Now I understand poverty-stricken, and now I know what I'm missing: freedom from black clouds that I cannot manage, freedom from helplessness and frustration because there is no getting ahead. But even worse are the hopelessness and depression that have begun to set in because, while I was once sure that securing adequate employment was just a matter of time, I now see no end to our economic deprivation. I see what has happened to other people, and I know that it can happen to me. My sense of security, derived from a higher source, has been overwhelmed by events, and I experience fear because I'm human and imperfect.

Being poor - "having little in the way of wealth, goods, or means of subsistence" - doesn't have to be devastating, though. Doing without luxuries is not a catastrophe. There are ways and means to run a household on a modest income, ask anyone of the older generation and they'll confirm it. Being poor can even be an effective teaching tool in the transmission of solid values to the younger generation. Even a man of little income who knows how to live frugally and sensibly and is willing to curtail his expectations can gain something over a life time, even if it were no more than the satisfaction of knowing that he paid his own way because he was willing to live within his means. But society must be willing to pay him sufficiently for his labors and, - and this is the crux of the matter, - **he has to be in control of his expenses.** Without adequate health insurance, though, he is not in control of his expenses; instead, he is dependent on the mercy of chance and government programs. It undermines his dignity and self-esteem. Through his payment of taxes he is forced to provide health insurance for many people who are better off than he, is left without enough income to take care of himself and his family and is reduced to begging, adding insult to injury. Such conditions do not promote "domestic tranquility and general welfare," something the U.S. constitution claims to "insure" and "promote."

Life is a challenge, and challenges we need if we are to grow and evolve. But if the struggle for physical survival takes up all of a man's energies then he has no energy left for his personal and spiritual development. The prevailing social attitudes have very effectively prevented him from pursuing his need and his right to evolve. The existing social order has become the enemy within.

Mother's Day, Shopping Day

It is that time of year again when duty to Mother obliges us to honor her. We do this the same way we honor past presidents in February, and the way we honor the birth of Christ in December - we go shopping.

My parish community's show of appreciation for its mothers was more gracious. It presented me with a flower as I walked into church. It made me feel uncomfortable, though, because I could not shake the feeling that compulsory attention to Mother on Mother's Day implies dispensation for the other 364 days.

Miss Anna Jarvis of Philadelphia originated the idea of a special Mother's Day in 1908. She did this out of a deep sentiment for her own mother. Six years later, in 1914, Congress signed a bill, J.J. Rs. 263, "designating the second Sunday in May as Mother's Day, and for other purposes, and making it the duty of the President to request its observance as provided for in this resolution."

There is something strange about a society that mandates the appreciation of its Mothers, which should be a natural and spontaneous attitude. It became an obligatory cause for shopping instead. What a burden for young children who think they have to buy something for their Mothers yet have no means to do so!

I see it this way: as a mother, I have an obligation to my children, and in rearing them I am simply doing my duty just as every member of society has a duty to perform. I am also fulfilling an obligation to my parents, grandparents and all the generations before them who struggled for survival and continuity. For my motherhood I expect nothing more than that my children treat me with the respect and consideration that every human being is entitled to – every day of the year. If I treat my mother well all year, what need is there for a gift? And if I do not treat her well all year, how meaningful is a gift on Mother's Day?

Cool Parkas

From time to time I have one of those discussions with my ten-year old son that frustrate him because instead of succeeding to manipulate me into compliant answers, he ends up with unanswerable questions from me. Of course I don't pose questions that he cannot answer, it's just that answering truthfully will wreak havoc with his desires and he cannot get what he wants. The worst of it is that he ends up spoiling his own argument. It goes something like this:

"Mom, can I have a parka?"

"When you need a new coat we'll talk about it."

"But everybody has a parka."

"Oh, you want a uniform, do you?" My son responds with a slight grin.

"Everybody in fifth grade has a parka," he insists.

"So, parkas are fifth grade uniforms. But since you are going into sixth grade we better find out what sixth grade uniforms are going to be." Another grin.

Then he says, "And you don't even have to zip it up; it slides right over your head."

"You already have such a piece of clothing. It's called a sweatshirt. But you never wear it." Agony spreads across his face. Then I say, "How would it be if I made a little sign that says: "This is a parka" and attach it to your sweatshirt. Would that work?" The agony spreads to his body that twists and squirms as though trying to get away from something painful.

"Nooo...! The parka I want has (sports team name) on it, right here on the sleeve, and on the back, and here in the front." My son points to all the appropriate places.

"Those are expensive. Why don't we just get an inexpensive parka, without names and emblems and all that stuff."

"But they're not cool," he answers. There's distress in his voice.

"Suppose I buy the parka you like, will the (sports team name) pay me for advertising it?"

"I don't think so," he replies vaguely, and hopelessness is spreading over his face.

"So you want me to pay a lot of money to this team and make it even richer than it already is, while I don't even know how I'm going to pay for the snow tires I need?"

"No, I guess not," he says with a sigh, and with his head drooping he slinks off to his room.

.

WEIMAR

Travel in the former East Germany

Die Wende, meaning "the turn, or change," is the German word for the process of Germany's reunification. It began with the fall of the Berlin Wall in November 1989 and was completed with combined national elections on October 3, 1990.

In July 1991, I traveled by fast Intercity train, named Johann Sebastian Bach, from my home town Fulda in Hessen, which is known to the American Military as the Fulda Gap, to Weimar in Thueringen, ca. 150 kilometers to the East. Before World War II direct railroad connections had existed between many towns and cities of these two neighboring states, but the Iron Curtain had done away with most of them. Consequently, centuries of fruitful human relations in the ancient volcanic massif, called RHOEN, which straddles the three states of Hessen, Thueringen and Bayern, had come to an abrupt end.

Now Germany was one again, but the severed highways and railways had not yet been reconnected and I was forced to travel the way of the last forty-five years, by way of Bebra to the North, and then East from there. Some travel from West to East had existed during the years of Communist control, but it had been made so complicated and so selective by East German authorities that few Westerners ever made the trip.

I was curious to know how I would recognize the point at which the train entered the former East German territory. When we came to Herleshausen, the former highway border crossing point, one of very few along the entire 858 mile length of the border, I knew. The train was spewing smoke now, yet it had started out with an electric engine since all of West Germany's railroad system is electrified. What's more, for some reason we were moving very slowly and the two conductors, a man and a woman, could not or would not tell me why. They had about them a curtness and sullenness that reminded me of Hollywood clichés of iron curtain residents, and the seeming truth of the cliché made me laugh.

Eisenach followed, an old industrial city where my father once had completed his apprenticeship in the hardware business. I was surprised at the beauty and grace of the townhouses that I could see from my window. Not that I could identify any particular architectural style. They were charming in their rich decorations, but, like beautiful children covered in dirt and rags so stood these stately homes covered in soot and decay. And if Herleshausen hadn't made me know that I had entered East German soil Eisenach surely did. Huge, ugly tenement buildings without style or grace followed, less sooty because less old but with the same air of indifference and neglect about them.

Leaving Eisenach, the train chugged along into the Thucringian Forest. It's not a very impressive region of rolling hills, not very high, not particularly beautiful, a region of vast mixed woodlands of the kind one reads about in fairy tales, where the hero walks for days without ever coming out of the trees. Among the rolling hills I discovered the famous Wartburg ruin where St. Elizabeth once reigned and cared for the poor. Legend has it that her husband did not approve of his wife's charitable work. He caught her once with a basket of food, hidden under her cloak, and demanded to know what she carried. She replied that she had flowers. Since it was winter her husband didn't believe her. When he took the basket from her, however, he discovered that it was filled with roses.

The hills disappeared in the distance again and the land spread out flat as a table. We passed through several hamlets. Rows of gardens with garden sheds were lined up along the railroad tracks. I learned later that owning such a garden was almost the only way in which an Easterner could escape city life for recreation and relaxation. Now and then I noticed a pipeline, consisting of a smaller one atop a larger one, with a total of perhaps four to five feet in height. They were following along the tracks, sometimes nearer, sometimes farther away and then disappearing altogether.

Groettstaedt, Gotah, Neudietendorf..... The hills returned and an occasional fortress or monastery ruin, a country road cobbled in the flat-topped coarse-grained square stones I knew from my youth, very little traffic, and always and everywhere the same slow little East-German car known as Trabant, but called by Westerners with affection and condescension "Trabbi," meaning to trot. Erfurth came next, a well known town of culture and early industry with a very peculiar cathedral that I knew from books.

Weimar was only 15 minutes away. It is a city of 61.500 people and was founded around 1250. The tracks were electrified now, the smoke from the front of the train had stopped. We had switched from an electric engine to a diesel engine and back again and I had never noticed it. For some reason, this 150 km trip, taken in a fast Intercity train, had taken almost three hours while it could have been done in half that time. On my arrival in Weimar I questioned the conductor, a different man, and I learned that the existing railway system was very much in need of repairs and, in many places, not safe enough for great speeds.

Weimar, the home and domain of poets and thinkers, composers and architects. Franz Liszt, Lucas Cranach, and Johann Sebastian Bach had worked here. In 1772, Duchess Anna Amalia had summoned the poet Christoph Martin Wieland, and in 1775, her husband, Duke Carl August, had invited Johann Wolfgang von Goethe who found in Weimar as poet, artist, researcher, and statesman a great field of activity and the creative power for his work. In 1776, the poet and philosopher Johann Gottfried von

Herder was brought on a recommendation by Goethe. In 1787, the poet Friedrich Schiller came for a temporary stay that became permanent in 1799. His dramas were produced by Goethe in the theater that the latter directed himself. The famous friendship between Goethe and Schiller became Weimar's crowning glory. After the classical period, a number of important schools brought new cultural impetus, among them an art college, a school for arts and crafts, the famous Bauhaus school of architecture, and a college for music.

Two months before my journey to Weimar I wrote to its mayor and asked to be put in touch with someone who would be willing to share with me some thoughts about life in the former DDR (German Democratic Republic). That is how I became acquainted with Baerbel (an affectionate form of Barbara), a middle aged lady who used to teach German culture and language to foreign students at the University of Rostock. Her daughter, a law student at the Potsdam University, happened to be present during my stay, and her young viewpoints were to add another dimension to my explorations.

They came to pick me up at the station, located not in the heart of historical Weimar but at its periphery - a form of city planning that had been used in many other German cities as well. The ladies took me to their apartment, located in a fairly new tenement building of perhaps 20 apartments, at the edge of town. Six or seven other buildings of equal size were located nearby. There were no sidewalks and only a hand-full of parking spaces. The rest of the grounds consisted of rock and earth piles of greater or smaller size. No landscaping existed; only a few trees had been planted near one building. A similar set of pipes as those that I had observed from the train had wound their way all the way from town to this hillside apartment complex and it turned out to be the water main for this housing project. Putting it underground was considered too costly. Then I noticed another building, smaller then the rest. It was designated as the school for this residential area, but since lack of funds prevented the completion of the playground, the school was not in use.

After freshening up, we all went downtown Weimar to go sightseeing. The name Weimar, incidentally, was chosen by Germany for the new republic which emerged from the collapsed empire in 1918, at the end of World War I. Germany intended to move away from the military image of the past toward the cultural image represented by Weimar. Tragically, though, the constitution of the Weimar Republic, modeled after the U.S. constitution, contained some important flaws, which later helped to propel a much needed unifying force, which happened to be Hitler, to power.

Historical Weimar contains a number of significant buildings and institutions. The national theater was being renovated, so I was not able to see the famous statue of Goethe and Schiller, united in a handshake of friendship, which is located in front of the theater complex. A lot of street repairs caused some traffic confusion. At a closer look I discovered that the sidewalks were being cobbled with small square stones, by hand, in the same patterns I remembered from my childhood. This was not, as I learned, a primitive attempt to cope without machinery but the result of a new, comprehensive plan to preserve the flavor of this city which plans to become European cultural center by 1999. Why such an odd-numbered year? In 1999, several round anniversaries will occur of important historical figures and events, such as Goethe's 250th birthday, Schiller's 240th birthday, and several others.

Lunchtime drew near and I was anxious to sample the local cuisine. We went to a restaurant which had just recently been reopened and which did not yet have the "licked" appearance, as Baerbel put it, of the West German establishments. Our meal of potato pancakes, sausages, and mixed vegetables was delicious and modestly priced. My friend Baerbel explained that this and many restaurants, and other businesses as well, had been closed because with prices dictated - and frozen - by the state, and raw materials always scarce there were never enough resources for adequate maintenance. The situation got so bad that people turned private property over to the state; there came a time even when the state, or the city, would no longer accept property.

Around three o'clock we were in the Goethe Haus, the home of Johann Wolfgang von Goethe who had actually been born in Frankfurt/Main. Goethe had hoped to become a positive influence in the culture of Weimar and Thueringen. Duke Carl August, however, who had persuaded him to come, could not justify simply keeping a poet and, therefore, gave him a court appointment and with it a place to live: the Goethe Haus. It began to rain heavily while touring it, but the little cafe inside the museum building, meant only for touring museum visitors, provided good coffee and excellent thueringian pastries, and the rain stopped when we were ready to leave.

The Schiller Haus was next on the agenda. It was more modest in its size and furnishings but just as vividly provided a taste of life in the 18th century. We came across a very peculiar little stool, and when I carefully tilted it sideways to check out its underside a lady employee "watchdog" of the museum - and there was at least one on every floor - barked at me rather angrily for touching the object. Baerbel was embarrassed that a foreign visitor was treated with such discourtesy, and she explained to me that many valuable museum pieces had been stolen since the Wende, probably to supply a lucrative underground market.

We decided to take a walk through the Park An Der Ilm (park on the river Ilm). This park was unlike the grand formal gardens of city castles; it was modeled after the natural gardens of the English countryside. In it stood a tall, unusually large garden house that had been given to Goethe when he had first arrived in Weimar. The park also contained a statue of William Shakespeare because Weimar has been seat of the German Shakespeare society since 1864. Weimar became seat of the Goethe society since its founding in 1886. But why was there a soviet cemetery in this park? Since Soviet military personnel came from far flung regions of the Soviet Union shipping bodies home was considered too problematic. Instead, they were buried on foreign soil, in the park in Weimar. A kind of posthumous public relations act, it occurred to me, since military personnel were always kept isolated from the civilian population.

After leaving the park we came past many other splendid buildings, most of them looking fairly presentable, but one of them, the state library, had totally deteriorated and its roof had caved in. Baerbel informed me that the historic heart of Weimar had been a showpiece for visiting Communist dignitaries of other Communist countries, and for that reason had been kept in reasonably good condition. I wondered, however, why the state library and not some other building had been allowed to disintegrate, and who would have been the one to make the decision to let it happen - East German or Soviet personnel. Baerbel did not have an answer, but in talking about German literature I discovered that certain epochs of German history and anything in literature that was perceived to be glorifying anti-Communist ideology had been systematically suppressed, had never been taught to her as a student, and in turn had not been taught by her as a teacher.

We left town, riding in Baerbel's car, which she had purchased in the West soon after the Wende, and drove to castle Belvedere. Along the way we passed an unfinished hotel that had been started before the Wende and was still not completed because the built-in electronic listening devices had yet to be removed.

The castle served as a temporary home to the mayor of Weimar and not much could be seen other than the outside. Here, also, existed a beautiful garden adjacent to an impressive greenhouse that was actually part of the south wing. The garden contained many plants that had been brought from foreign countries long ago, among them ginkgo trees, the oldest living species of tree, and a number of palm trees in large attractive and permanent containers which could be wheeled in and out of the greenhouse according to seasonal need.

From the East end of the garden we had a grand view of the country, still very much covered in Germany's characteristic mixed woods of deciduous and coniferous trees - majestic beech and oak trees, focus of worship by ancient tribes; towering ash trees with a clump of branches way up high; great spruces with the sinister feel of Grimm's fairy tales; lovely linden trees with their fragrant aroma, German folk music's focus and symbol of lovers' sad farewells. I stood and pondered the great expanse of trees and I felt that the poet Eichendorff must have stood here and seen what I saw because his words, set to music by the composer Mendelssohn, suddenly echoed in my mind: "Oh Taeler weit, oh Hoehen, oh schoener gruener Wald...."Oh valleys wide, oh highlands, oh beautiful green woods who are the rapt abode of my joys and sorrows...." And the poet and the composer and I were one in the knowledge of that ceaseless yearning for oneness that draws the German soul to its beloved forest.

On our way back to Baerbel's apartment we stopped once more to buy some chocolates from an obviously new and flashy sweets shop. Baerbel and her daughter Dorothea beamed with pleasure at being able to afford what had once been a prohibitively priced luxury item. On a nearby house wall was scribbled, "Kohl (chancellor of a united Germany) has betrayed you."

Back at the apartment, Baerbel showered, and then we all got comfortable in the living room with a bottle of Pacific NW wine that I had brought as a gift for my hostess.

Dorothea began telling of her life as a law student, which was not too different from an American student's life. She had the same problems with lack of affordable housing close to the university, heavy traffic in Potsdam near Berlin, a needed part-time job to help pay for living expenses, for even though tuition is free, living is not. Her biggest aggravation, however, although she took it in stride, was the loss of almost two years of law credits because East German law was now obsolete.

Her mother had different concerns: that her rent of one hundred Deutsche Mark for her city-owned two-bedroom apartment might now, as a result of the newly adopted free enterprise system, rise by as much as four hundred percent. For reasons that were not explained to me, she could no longer work as a teacher, and no other employment seemed available to her at the age of fifty-five. It was a bewildering situation for a member of a society that no longer existed, which had actually created jobs where not enough work existed so that all people could be guaranteed an income. This policy had fostered a deplorable work ethic among many East Germans. Baerbel, like all women, had always worked at an outside job (if there was nothing to do, knitting socks was allowed) while being a homemaker. She resented the West's image of an inferior the East German worker. Our conversation ended when some American detective crime story on TV took hold of their attention.

While getting ready for bed I had opportunity to examine the structural aspects of the apartment. The concrete walls of this prefabricated building were probably no more than two inches thick and had no sound insulation. Some of the doors, which looked like lids on cardboard boxes, opened into the rooms and some doors opened outward. All door openings lacked moldings; consequently, the wallpaper reached to the very edge of the door opening and was, therefore, subject to immediate peeling and cracking.

All plumbing and wiring was installed above the walls. The toilet sat too far from the wall, the bathtub and basin, situated side by side, shared one faucet with a long swivel spout. A plain concrete balcony lacked all finishing touches. The furniture was made of pressed and laminated boards, but my bed for the night was very comfortable. Despite its shortcomings, this apartment exuded the same orderliness, attractiveness and care that is typical of German homes.

Breakfast the next morning took place in the kitchen. German rooms have no closets - clothes are kept in wardrobes - and can therefore serve as either bedrooms or dining rooms according to need and preference. After breakfast Baerbel and I went downtown again while her daughter stayed behind to prepare for her own drive back to Potsdam later that day.

We drove to the railroad station first, to stow away my luggage in a rental storage box, and then we strolled through town again. I noticed a pregnant young woman and realized that I had seen no others. Another bit of graffiti read - "Ruin that which ruins you." A little later, another slogan - "Away with Nazis." We came to an old cemetery that had been allowed to "re-naturalize." It is a program of allowing nature to go its way by not interfering unnecessarily with growth of grasses, etc., something I had observed in parks and cemeteries of the West as well.

One of the dukes of Weimar, a Roman Catholic, had married the sister of a Russian Tsar who was Russian Orthodox. At the time of their deaths, the respective churches felt obliged to bury each one according to their faith, yet side-by-side. It was accomplished in the following way. A small Roman Catholic church and a small Russian Orthodox church were built side-by-side with their walls joined, but separate on the inside. The crypts, however, are open to each other and there, where the two churches above are joined, lie the two sarcophagi side by side. This little church, which probably doesn't hold more than 20 people, is the only Russian Orthodox church in existence in the area, and it was used for services by the Soviet soldiers who were stationed in Weimar. I never saw any of them, never saw any evidence of a foreign presence at all, other than the cemetery in the Park On The Ilm. Baerbel told me that it is, and always has been, Soviet policy to keep the occupation forces isolated from the civilian population. (They would leave with pomp and ceremony on November 21, 1992.)

The time came for Baerbel to run some errands and for me to get back to the station. She took me to the proper streetcar, we said good-bye, promised to write, and off I went to catch a train for Erfurth.

Leaving the train in Erfurth, I felt like entering a time warp, so much resembled this station those which I had regularly traversed on my way to and from boarding school in the West during the 1950s. There were the same sooty, soiled and pock-marked tiled underground passages from the platforms to the terminal. The existence of 1., 2., and 3. class restaurants, which corresponded to 1., 2., and 3. class modes of travel of long ago, amazed me considering the professed classlessness of the Communist ideology. I saw the same barely acceptable restrooms for men and women, separated by a small room between them where a caretaker in a white lab coat made change that was needed for the use of the facilities. There was grass, no a meadow growing on the roof of the freight depot. Hotel Erfurth faced the southern rim of the station square. It was a large attractive building although sooty from years of diesel exhaust, and pink flowers growing in window boxes were a pathetic attempt to add some beauty. What appeared to be a main street, and indeed turned out to be a rather dull shopping street, led past the hotel, and I decided to follow it.

While looking for a streetcar that could take me from the station to the famous cathedral I encountered a political demonstration. Crowds had blocked the tracks, and after asking the distance to the church I decided to walk. The stores I passed were few, and anything other than arts and crafts left much to be desired in styling, quantity and, I would presume, quality as well. For years, the best of East German products had been sold to the West for hard currency while East Germans had to get by with few inferior products. Three times I came across the outline of a human body, painted onto the sidewalk as though felled by a bullet, with a number above 1100 painted inside the outline. When I asked about it I was told that the number represented the number of workers that had lost their jobs with IG Metall, a large and powerful German corporation.

The cathedral turned out to be an intriguing combination of differing architectural styles, built, added onto, renovated, and expanded ever since the year 752. And in the peculiar logic of the middle ages a second church had been erected right beside it, no more than fifty yards away.

When my feet began to ache I decided to rest myself awhile with a good cup of coffee. The West has many pleasant little cafes but in Erfurth they were hard to come by. Finally, getting a bit desperate, I entered the dining room of the impressive Gildehaus (house of guilds). It has interior decor of serious elegance dating back to 1584, and here I was served coffee and pastry. A little later, with renewed vigor, I began to probe the many side streets, less important churches, river and bridges while working my way back toward the station.

When I reached the station with time to spare I had no wish to see anymore. For more than five hours I had walked through Erfurth, and now I was not simply tired but rather emotionally exhausted. I felt a physical revulsion against the sensation that I had swallowed every bit of dirt, soot, grime, and pollution that my eyes had seen that afternoon. Erfurth had obviously not been a showpiece for visiting Communist party dignitaries, and the neglect and decay was appalling. I had seen townhouses with their roofs caved in and upper floors unlivable while the street level was still inhabited. Piecemeal repair work, when it existed at all, had lost out against the utter frustration, despair, stoicism, and finally indifference that had set in among a people who had once taken great pride in their physical surroundings. The same question, one that Baerbel had not been able to answer, kept crossing my mind: who or what were the forces which caused a government of Germans, answerable to Moskow though they had been, but German nonetheless, to systematically destroy German values and ideals. Was it really nothing else than the economic policy of central planning? Or was it that proletarians, not developed enough to appreciate higher values, threw out the baby with the bath water when they got rid of the nobility and the values it had signified?

Baerbel had related to me how very disappointing and painful the Wende with all its changes had been for her who had so very much believed in solidarity with other Communist countries, something that had been preached to her since childhood. And how can anyone object to the ideal of solidarity which is simply another word for brotherhood. But it seemed to me that clever proletarians had exploited people and country under the guise of brotherhood while at the same time condemning the aristocracy for committing the same sin under a different guise. But the nobility, guilty though some of them had been of forgetting that true nobility is wisdom, honor, and compassion, had left behind a legacy of high art and high ideals. Communism had left nothing but a cadaver.

The Alarming Finality
of RIGHT and WRONG

Recently, I had opportunity to talk to a priest of an Orthodox Church regarding its origin and split from a dissenting group. The priest was a sociable, outgoing young man of modern pragmatic attitudes as he carried about his baby in an infant-carrying contraption strapped to his chest. He explained to me the differences in their theological views, and in doing so he labeled the opposing view as "wrong." He used this word with such sureness, such unequivocal conviction of knowing that it caught my attention because of its alarming finality. With sureness of conviction that the other group was wrong he implied, with the same conviction, that his group was right.

For many years now, I've been leaning toward a more open and flexible view of life and its meaning. It literally startled me, therefore, to discover that in this day and age there are still elements that are so dogmatic about matters which are neither in the realm of the empirical nor are fully known and/or understood. Every church admits that it doesn't know some things, that this and that cannot be explained and that faith has to enter where reason cannot prevail.

In all my questions about life, whether material or spiritual, I have noticed a helpful parallel in the institution of the family. A three-year-old thinks that his father is the biggest and smartest man there ever was and that his town is the whole world. His viewpoint is limited, and we know that as he grows older he will know better. And when the child is four years old and attempts to draw a horse that turns out to look like a pig, a wise parent will praise the child for its efforts and will agree that it was, indeed, a very good horse. The point is: four year olds are incapable of drawing recognizable horses, but if the child attempts to draw a horse, believes that it has drawn a horse, then indeed it did so.

In the same way, I believe, our views of God and spirituality are never either right or wrong but simply evidence of a given stage of development. As children, we think of God as a father, an authority figure who sits on a throne and judges right and wrong, and that's all right, because in childhood - and I mean physical childhood as well as spiritual childhood - we have limited comprehension and knowledge. When we get older, our knowledge of life broadens and our view of God changes, and rightfully so. And if we have no views of God at all then that's all right too, for if God is unimaginable, then no one can imagine what or how he is, and the one who thinks he has found him has actually lost him because he stops looking for him. Everyone's perception of God and the purpose of life is based on the individual's particular set of experiences and knowledge. No one has the absolute truth, but everyone has a bit of it.

Trouble will ensue, though, when a person begins to act on his convictions at insufficient stages of development, and we can see this very clearly when verbal protest turns into physical abuse. During my childhood, to be wrong was almost tantamount to being criminal. Protestants were wrong, therefore, we Catholics stayed away from them. Divorced people were wrong and therefore shunned. The man who didn't work extra hours but, instead, took extra vacations, was wrong and was looked on with suspicion. Everybody who had different views from the prevailing ones of a particular group was wrong and therefore suspect. There was never any middle ground, only right and wrong, and we were taught early on, explicitly or implicitly, to turn away from people who are wrong and therefore guilty. The resultant devastating antagonisms all around the world are well known and documented. But the worst part of this attitude is that when we believe to be right we stop searching for the truth and thereby close ourselves off to greater knowledge and deeper understanding. Our belief system remains stunted. This condition of stunted growth causes us to turn away from ourselves as well, and we suffer from guilt and shame after having done wrong because we associate our mistakes with sin in all its ominous interpretations, instead of seeing our mistakes as consequences of inadequate development, a weakness that can be overcome with time and determination. No healthy one-year old was ever deterred from mastering walking, regardless of falls and bruises and pain. No human being will fail to reach perfection when desire and will prevail, regardless of falling short, not measuring up, and the pain that comes from it.

All eternity is spent in the pursuit of perfection in its many aspects: perfect love, perfect compassion, perfect knowledge etc. It takes many, many lives to get there, and everyone has to do it in his own way and in his own time. There are a great number of variables involved in the make-up of every personality, variables of genetic make-up, cultural and social heritage, race, physical body characteristics, family, teachings, religion, previous lifetimes with their unimaginable store of experiences. Even those of us who don't believe in reincarnation must admit that the variables of just one lifetime are enough to give each person a completely different outlook on life and the human condition. It doesn't make sense to think that anyone of us can know the whole truth, or that any one group possesses it while, therefore, everybody else must be wrong.

All life is Devine, however undeveloped it may be. If we would understand that to be human is a process of becoming, if we could see the human condition as an ongoing developmental process at varying stages of proficiency rather than being finished or unfinished, right or wrong, then we would be more tolerant of those who have not yet reached a high level of development. In other words, we wouldn't chide someone for not living up to our expectations. We would have more tolerance and patience with our own shortcomings as well, and without the debilitating effects of shame and guilt and recriminations for being wrong we would make faster progress in our development toward our goal of perfection.

My Pet Peeve

If I had power to do one great thing I would get rid of the advertisement industry. Yes, of course, they have valid arguments for their existence – we might only buy what we need if it were not for the ads. Once in a while, I gladly admit, an ad comes along that is quite entertaining and clever. But for the most part, they are dumb, banal, violent, suggestive, boring, downright annoying, or all of the above.

If the ads were designed to simply sell a given product, there would be no objection. But they do much more than that; with much clever deception and misinformation they actually corrupt the human person and its intrinsic value. It started out innocently enough in the fashion ads, for instance, with the accentuation of a model's given physical aspect. Over time, accentuation became exaggeration and, finally, outright corruption. Fashion models became ever thinner, taller, lankier. Recently, I checked out the latest fashion catalog from a prominent store, and I would have laughed if it hadn't been so sad. Across the pages parade females with facial expressions from dumb to confused to childish, wearing little girl frocks, having style-less long hair, no breasts or hips to speak of, skinny long legs made to appear even longer by wearing three-inch high heels. These are women? The sum total of this pre-teen gawkiness is focus and fodder for pedophiles.

At the other end of the extreme, ad agencies present females with a breast implant or two, immature hips and long bony legs. Brainwashed people call this model a sexy female. Her immature hips promise no pregnancy and her artificially big breasts do not suggest infant nurturing. This female is not a woman. She is a toy for boys with homosexual tendencies

Deadly Consequences

Some day, long before I'm old and decrepit, and long before my mind is ready to retire, and while my limbs are still straight and strong, watching the daily news on television is going to kill me.

I'm a sensitive person who feels the pain of others and emphasizes with the challenges, dilemmas, and vanities of the human race. As a matter of fact, I become totally absorbed in the stories that are presented by the newscasters, but because they hurry to proclaim the awful headlines, and because they don't seem to know the meaning of a comma or period and therefore cram one sentence into the next one and one story into the next one without any sort of signal like momentarily lowering their eyes, or making a pause, or taking a breath, or changing their facial expression to indicate that one sentence has ended and the next is beginning, or that one story, perhaps amusing, is ending and the next, perhaps tragic, is beginning, I get pulled along and dragged out to near fatal loss of oxygen which is only prevented by my husband's occasional comment or the tricky leg support of my rocking chair which likes to collapse on me from time to time and startles my consciousness back into the here and now, and sometimes it's the annoying phone call from a pesky marketer that keeps me from getting so totally sucked into the cyber world of human affairs that I stop breathing.

But some day, long before I'm old and decrepit, and long before my mind is ready to retire, and while my limbs are still straight and strong, watching the daily news on television, I fear, is going to kill me.

Political Correctness

Some elements denounce the music
composed by Richard Wagner
'cause man and music, so they say,
are infamously racist.

If that's the logic, then denounce
the American constitution
because its writers were involved
and practiced subjugation.

Hot Crow

How hot the summer sun does seep
through feathers, black, that seize the heat
Through leath'ry socks into my feet
And through the nostrils in my beak.

Water, water everywhere
But not a drop to drink.

It's chlorinated – yukk – by rules
It's dirty, hot in stagnant pools
It's cooked to tea in people's gutters
It's spoiled by gas and oil from sputters
There are some birdbaths here and there
With water, fresh, when people care
But cats are roaming high and low
To pounce upon unlucky crow.

Water, water everywhere
Is there no drop to drink?

But ah, there is, I found at last
on shopping street and right near Max
A basin, off the ground for ease
Just right the rim for my big feet
To sit in comfort while I drink
From people's bubbling water sink.
It gushes up from deep inside
So clear and bright, a joy for eyes.

Water, water everywhere
And lots of drops to drink.

I'm Getting Old

It's true. My body tells me so every day. And why not! Already, I'm several years past that magic number sixty-five, which is the beginning of what social and political correctness call the Golden Years. That's a deceptive phrase, designed to distract from the true events of that time in life - high blood pressure, high cholesterol, aching joints, sagging this, drooping that... the list goes on. That lovely sounding term also pretends to add value to the oldster's existence, which has become all but valueless in a society that worships youth and immaturity.

No, I'm not "getting on in years," I'm not "past my prime," I'm not mature, venerable or senior – I am old, and I have acquired the nonchalant honesty and audacity to prove it. Sometimes, when the urge to prick someone's composure comes over me, I tell them that I am old. I do this – oh, I'm so bad – because it's fun to watch how their facial expressions suddenly change and their bodies begin to squirm. It causes some people real anxiety because calling someone old is socially incorrect. Those who would agree with my statement find themselves in a real dilemma: if they agree that I am old, and if they say so out loud, they risk offending me. If they say nothing, a tense and awkward silence will ensue, which they cannot tolerate for fear that I will interpret it as an agreement and, again, they risk offending me. Those who cannot even bear to consider the word old lest they be reminded of their own future fate, will hasten to assure me that I am not old at all. In order to lend credence to their statement they qualify it by telling me why they think that I am not old - because I look much younger than my age, they might say. However true or false it might be, nothing changes the fact that I have lived a certain number of years and am, therefore, old.

I don't mind getting old because the older I get the more I learn. Knowledge is its own reward. No longer do I suffer from those dreadful feelings of inadequacy and inferiority that used to plague me when I was young and ignorant and thought that everybody else knew everything, only I knew nothing. No longer do I have to heed what others tell me because I can find the truth for myself. I have learned to discriminate between choices and am confident in the decisions I make. Would I prefer being young, beautiful and ignorant? No way.

No, I don't mind getting old, but I do mourn the loss of beauty. I mourn the loss of my slender youthful body that was once covered in flawless taut skin. I feel sad when I look at old photographs and see just how much my body has aged since my youth, when I didn't dare think of myself as being beautiful but now realize that I was. I regret the loss of healthy teeth and flexible joints and perfect vision. And just because I know that all other living things start out fresh and beautiful (except naked mole rats) only to lose out in the end, it does nothing to alleviate my very personal pain.

Knowing that some day I will have another new, perfect body doesn't help either because it, too, will wilt and wither away. But some day – I use "day" for lack of a better term; time has no meaning in real life - some day, when I have sufficiently evolved, I will be at One with all the beauty in existence at that time or place or in that condition. I will be at One with it. I will take it all in like the drop takes in the ocean. And it will never be lost to me because I'll no longer be burdened with a physical body that all too soon gets restless and bored with anything lasting too long, even beauty and perfection. Until then, biding my time is my only option, but while I'm waiting I will continue to evolve and grow in love, knowledge and wisdom. That is, after all, the reason for living.

Samie and the Auto Dealer

Samuel was a slight young man, short and thin, with feet and ears that were too large for his body. His face was round and bony; there was very little flesh on it. His kinky hair stood thick and high off his meager face, was flat where he had slept on it and dented where a cap had pressed its rim into it. His skin was deep brown, almost black, and was sprinkled with irregular sized spots that might have been considered freckles on a white skin. His total appearance lacked anything of interest, yet despite his short frame he stood tall and straight, his head held proud and high, and he moved with the calm grace and fluidity that exemplify many native Africans. Like most young men from Africa, he had come to the USA for an education and, unlike some young men from Africa, he was looking forward to going back to his native Sudan to help better the lives of his countrymen. In his deep brown eyes burned the fire of noble ambition.

Samie, as he liked to be called, shared a basement apartment with a student from Chad by the name of Ennedi. It was located in a small town at the outskirt of a larger town where the two African students attended Community College. They had part-time jobs in a lumberyard that was one half hour drive from their apartment. Ennedi gave Samie rides to the College and took him along to work. He drove an old Honda that shook and rattled fearfully and made Samie worry that any time now the car would heave its last breath, and he, Samie, would not get to work and therefore lose income. When Ennedi found a better paying job as a milker on a large dairy farm Samie was forced to hitchhike to work. After he spent several days in great anxiety over the unreliability of his transportation, he found a man who owned an old car and, as luck would have it, worked in the same lumberyard and promised him rides. This driver turned out to be half mad, though. At top speed, he raced along the two-lane road, around sharp turns, up and down steep dips in the road, and he overtook anything in front of him regardless of visibility or the lack of it. Without benefit of seatbelts, Samie was tossed about like a salad in the passenger seat that had nothing for him to hold on to. Muddled and half senseless he arrived at the job site. It took a couple of hours before his jittery nerves had calmed down only to become agitated again at the prospect of the return trip.

Samie, who carefully clung to every dollar and never allowed himself any luxuries, decided to buy a car. In Sudan, owning a car was an unmistakable sign of success. Samie couldn't help but grin with self-conscious pride when he told Ennedi of his plan. Sudanese people had always looked to Europe for imports, and Samie knew that owning a Mercedes represented the height of earthly accomplishments. He was aware, of course, that he could not afford such a car, even a used one, and that he would probably never own one. When he came across a used Audi 100 at a price he could afford he decided to buy it. He felt very lucky indeed for he knew that Audis, too, were built in Germany and had a reputation for great quality.

Samie found this car at the town's most reputable dealership. He thought it superfluous to question the dealer about the quality of the car. He already knew of the Audi's reputation. Nonetheless, he asked questions, and the dealer remarked repeatedly, "there's not a damn thing wrong with it, not a damn thing."

Interest rates were very high at that time - seventeen, eighteen, even nineteen percent. Under such economic conditions, people shied away from buying cars. But Samie's auto dealer had become inventive. In order to sell cars, the dealer agreed to pay half the interest on a loan granted by an accommodating bank. The dealer related this fact to Samie, but Samie's English skills were not sufficient to understand sales and financing terminology. Ennedi had to fill him in. He went to the appointed bank, filled out the forms with Ennedi's help, and was granted the loan. Then the two Africans went back to the dealership and completed the purchase. Neither one of them noticed a peculiar grin that passed between the auto dealer and his assistant.

Ennedi, who had come along, drove the car to a large deserted lot nearby where he explained to Samie the tools of the driver. Samie caught on quickly and was able to drive the car back to their apartment, a few blocks away. Then Ennedi procured a driver's manual and read it to Samie. A whole new vocabulary opened up for him – not only new words, but phrases and concepts and signs that made no sense to him who had grown up in the African countryside without railroads, freeways and traffic signs.

With or without Ennedi, Samie spent every free moment studying the driver's manual and practicing driving by himself. He knew that the law required an experienced driver to be with him, but Ennedi was not always available. According to the way and culture in which Samie had grown up, he did what was necessary to accomplish what he needed to do.

What a nerve wrecking experience it turned out to be. It was one thing to sit in Ennedi's car as a passenger, looking out of the window and trying to guess at the agricultural products that lined the road on the way to work. It was something altogether different to be sitting behind the wheel of his own car, in motion, on the street, trying to recognize and interpret the meaning of traffic signs while English and his native Arabic wrestled for dominance in his head. While trying to sort out such linguistic muddles he inevitably drove right past the objects of his confusion.

Practice makes perfect, though. When Samie thought he was ready, Ennedi took him to the DMV. First came the oral part. The officer asked a question, when Samie wasn't sure he understood it Ennedi translated it into Arabic. Samie then answered in Arabic and then Ennedi translated it into English. The officer took it for granted that Ennedi translated the answer exactly as Samie gave it rather than fixing a wrong answer in the translation.

Samie was jubilant when he held his driver's license in his hand. It seemed a much greater achievement than getting a 3-point grade average at the Community College. His smile of pride and satisfaction nearly split his face in half and showed up two rows of regular white teeth. To celebrate his achievement, and to thank Ennedi for his help, Samie invited him to a dance bar later that evening. The two friends drank some sodas and danced a few times with local young women who did not smoke.

Samie could hardly wait to drive himself to school the next day. In Sudan, not owning a car was the norm for people. After coming to the US however, not owning a car had come to feel like a lack of something important, some knowledge that everyone else possessed except Samie. Every student who came to school by car knew about cars, had grown up with cars, and had early in life become intimate with the machine. Not only that, but owning a car afforded young Americans a great deal of freedom, more than most Sudanese would experience in an entire lifetime. Getting the money to pay for a car, even paying for repairs and insurance, all these matters comprised a realm of experience that Samie was lacking. It had made him feel incomplete. Now he was looking forward to experience that which Americans had long taken for granted.

Just for fun on that first day of ownership, Samie drove his own car instead of riding with Ennedi. He was nervous; but the route to the College was familiar now, and he was confident that he would not overlook any traffic signs. When he came to the last traffic signal before turning onto the College parking lot he stopped for the red light. When it changed to green and he gave gas, the car died.

Samie was dumfounded. The car behind him honked. He turned the ignition key, gave gas, banged on the dashboard in desperation but nothing happened. He tried this, that and the other, but not even a squeak could he get out of his Audi. Repeated impatient honking from behind made him nervous. He looked out of the window and gestured to the car behind him to pass. His look of helplessness caught the attention of a couple of students on foot. They came over and suggested that he put the car in neutral and stir it to the side of the road while they would push him. Samie was greatly relieved for this advice and did as he was told. Asking the students what might be the trouble with his car brought only a shrug from them, and they hurried off. Samie followed slowly, drudging as under a heavy load while his mind tried to come to grips with the first lesson of a sorely missed experience.

Later that morning he found Ennedi in the cafeteria and told him about the mishap. In talking about it he became agitated. He was so utterly confused that he couldn't think of what to do next. Ennedi offered him a ride back to the apartment, but to get to work Samie had to hitchhike again. Early on the following morning the two friends had the obstinate Audi towed back to the dealer. Samie told him that he wanted to return the car because there was a problem with it. The dealer assured him that "there is not a damn thing wrong with it, not a damn thing," and suggested that, perhaps, Samie didn't know how to treat the car, given that he was a foreigner who had had no experience with cars. Perhaps he had flooded it, the dealer said and climbed into the car, turned the ignition key and the motor started right up. With mouth agape and probably red-faced with embarrassment - if the color could have been detected - he thanked the dealer, got in his car and drove off.

Three days later, on his way to the lumberyard, the Audi stopped again. In the middle of nowhere, without any rhyme or reason, the motor simply quit. The car rolled a few more yards and then stopped altogether. Samie had the presence of mind to stir it as far off the road as was possible. He got out, confused, angry and frustrated, walked around the car, looked under the hood, knowing full well that it was useless, but he had to do something. As luck would have it, the mad driver came by. He slowed down long enough to recognize Samie who stood by the side of the road with a bewildered look on his face. Then he stopped, called out to Samie and offered him a ride. Samie took it gladly.

On the way to work he continually asked the mad driver what could be the matter with his Audi. Audis are great quality cars, he was sure of it, had heard it over and over from other people, from the television commercials, even from magazine articles. The mad driver just nodded, or shrugged; he was preoccupied with passing every car he came upon, never mind the double yellow lines that zoomed up and dashed past in a flash. For once Samie did not worry about his life for his thoughts were left behind in the inexplicable Audi.

Once again, Samie and Ennedi had the Audi towed, but this time directly to a garage. The mechanic looked it over briefly, listened to what Samie had to say about it, turned the ignition key without result, then said he would check it out and call him when he had a diagnosis. Meanwhile, Samie was reduced to the status of a passenger, which not only inconvenienced him but also bruised his newfound pride in success and ownership.

On the following morning, the mechanic called and told him what was wrong with the car, that he had fixed it, and that he could come pick it up. To answer Samie's question, the mechanic explained the problem, but Samie didn't understand any of it. Just glad to get his car back, although troubled by the money he would have to pay, he went and picked it up.

For three whole weeks, the Audi performed perfectly. It gave Samie some peace of mind, a chance to overcome the anxiety that had plagued him every time he got into the car since the first time the Audi had let him down. His optimism returned, his pride flourished – although more sedately - he even offered rides to other students.

On the Sunday following College break, Samie drove to a neighboring city, about one-hour drive away, to visit his cousin Akasha. This cousin had completed Community College and had moved on to the University where he studied mechanical engineering. The two-lane road passed through rolling hills of sagebrush, dotted here and there in valley-like depressions by farms whose surrounding acreages were irrigated from streams that flowed through the valleys. Just as he passed the city limits the Audi had a seizure. It hit Samie as with a punch in the beltline.

Again, Samie stood by the side of the road with a bewildered look on his face and again, a Good Samaritan offered help and drove him to a gas station from where Samie called his cousin. Why is this happening? Audis are supposed to be good cars! What's wrong with it? Why does it just stop while I'm driving? Samie overwhelmed his cousin with questions he could not answer. Finally, the cousin told Samie that he needed a proper mechanic, one who is trained in the repair of Audis and other foreign cars. He called a friend with whose help they towed the stranded Audi to a local garage. Money was flowing through Samie's hands like water. The visit with his cousin was soured by the growing Audi nightmare.

On Monday, the foreign car repair shop called and told Akasha that the car needed a new starter, some tightening here and there, and then it should be all right. He could come and pick it up by noon. With a heavy heart, Samie asked his cousin to lay out the money for him and he would pay him back. Then, after picking up the car, he drove back

Next morning, on getting into the Audi to go to school, near sick with worry, the engine said nothing - not a sputter, not a squeak, not even a whine. Samie, feeling sicker by the minute, walked around the car, opened the hood, slammed it down, kicked the tire. It seemed to him that this German auto acted very much like a Sudanese mule - stubborn, obstinate, not even to be moved with a kick in the rear. If he were a violent man he would take a whip and work off his frustration on the stubborn animal.

When he had a chance, Samie called his cousin and reported the latest Audi mishap. Akasha told him something he had kept from him to spare his feelings - the foreign car technician had said that he thinks this Audi had been wrecked and rebuilt and might never function properly. Samie was devastated. Not only had he lost his means of transportation, his self-esteem had suffered, his savings were gone, and he was forced to borrow to pay his bills. Borrowing money caused him almost more grief than the temperamental Audi. He felt as if he were standing at an abyss - there seemed to be no way forward. What to do?

In talking it over with Ennedi, Samie decided to return the car. He would not keep it. No way. But how does a poor African nobody force a reputable and prominent local American car dealer to take back a car? It seemed hopeless. The two friends began talking to other students about what car troubles they might have experienced and how they had dealt with them. They found out that the car dealer is required to note the odometer reading on the purchase agreement. Samie checked his papers; there was none. He felt a glimmer of hope. Then the two friends consulted a lawyer who came recommended from one of the students. Samie asked the lawyer if he, Samie, had a case against the auto dealer on the basis of the missing odometer reading. The lawyer said he would check it out and get back to him.

When he called the next day, he said that he could not take the case because his firm represented the auto dealer.

Samie didn't catch on, but Ennedi laughed and said, "did you get what just happened? You didn't know if you had a case or not. But the lawyer just gave away that you do have a case." Samie frowned; he could see no advantage in this fact.

"Don't you see? You can take the blasted Audi back to the dealer and ask for your money back."

"What if he doesn't take it back?"

"What else can he do if you leave this lemon in his garage," answered Ennedi.

"But what if he doesn't give me back my money? I can't force him to return my money, can I? And then I still have to make payments to the bank. Oh, damn, what a mess I got myself into."

For several days the Audi rested in the driveway, jarring Samie's ease whenever he came in sight of it. Every day he rode to work with the mad driver and came to think that his driving was not half as bad as the fact that he, Samie, had debts. When time for another loan payment came around he went to the bank and explained that the Audi he bought was in bad condition, that it had cost him a lot of money for towing and repairs. The bank agreed that Samie skip his payment and add it to the end of the contract period. Akasha thought it a remarkable gesture on the part of the bank. Banks were not known to be so generous. And although the bank held title to the car, the whole thing seemed rather unusual. Ennedi voiced the same sentiments.

When he got paid the next time, Samie had the car towed back to the dealer. The dealer seemed rather kind and showed much concern for Samie's troubles. When he had first come to buy, the dealer had acted indifferent as though he did not expect Samie to be a serious customer - a customer with money. Samie told the dealer to take back the car. The dealer began to complain of the bad times.

Samie hinted that the car might have been wrecked. The dealer proclaimed his business to be a highly respected one. Samie remarked that a dealer could surely afford the loss easier than a poor student. The dealer complained ever louder about the bad times and that he was losing his shirt in this business. It made Samie feel bad and less sure of his action.

Finally, the dealer suggested that Samie should take the car to a certain mechanic in town who had experience and training in the repair of foreign cars. He even offered to pay for half the repair and tow the car with his own tow truck. Samie was persuaded to try one more time.

The mechanic lived in town and not far from where Samie lived. He took in the Audi, and as they all did, he said he'd check it out and let him know what the problem is. And, yes, the dealer had called and informed him of the deal; Samie would only pay half the cost. At the word cost, Samie squirmed and almost regretted having agreed to this deal.

Two days later, after getting a call from the mechanic with a diagnosis, which Samie did not understand, he picked up the car. The cost was tolerable, but his disposition was one of extreme anxiety as he climbed into the car. He feared to turn the ignition key lest this feeble Audi would collapse once again. But it held. The motor sounded good – if he could be a proper judge of it. He left the garage, and on his way home stopped at a grocery store for some food items that he needed. When he returned, the Audi had fallen asleep and would not wake up.

Frustrated to the extreme, Samie walked all the way back to the garage and told there what happened. The garage owner was not present, and the mechanic tried to persuade him that whatever the problem, he could surely fix it, but Samie had had it. He insisted that a tow truck be called and the Audi be taken back to the dealer.

With the Audi back in the dealer's garage, Samie took the car keys, held them high for everyone to see, and said, "Here are the keys. I refuse to accept the Audi." With that, he dropped the keys on a counter and walked out.

Samie had missed work, but he didn't care. This mess had to be taken care of once and for all. It had made him feel proud, and he inwardly gloated that he, the poor African student was now calling the shots. When Ennedi returned home and Samie told him what he had done, he laughed and cheered him. But once again, the question arose of how to make the dealer return the money

"Let's see now," said Ennedi. "The dealer has the car but he can't sell it because the bank has the title – and the title is in your name! Oh, I know!!" he suddenly yelled all excited. "The dealer owes half the interest on the loan. If you don't pay, then the dealer has to make payments. Wow! That's how you're going to get him." And Ennedi danced about like a sparing boxer.

He had to explain again how it was possible for a poor student to beat a businessman at his own game. Finally, Samie understood. A powerful sense of righteous triumph came over him and filled him with a sense of satisfaction the likes of which he had never experienced in his life.

The dealer called and wanted to talk to Samie. Samie refused to take the call. He would not be cheated again. Since he still wanted, needed a car, Samie decided to offer the dealer a trade. The dealer should take back the Audi, and Samie would pick out another car. Samie put it in writing. It had become obvious to him that even a reputable businessman could not be trusted to tell the truth about his merchandise. Then he went back to the car dealership and presented his proposal, in writing.

The dealer agreed to the trade and signed the paper that Samie had prepared to that end. Then he checked out all the available cars and decided on a Ford Granada. This time, he drove it not just around the block, but out on the highway, and in town with many stops, to assure himself that the car would not die on him. Then it occurred to him that, perhaps, he could even have the car tested by an old mechanic by the name of Mac.

Through a social event at a local community action agency, Ennedi had become acquainted with Mac, a retired car mechanic who had worked on cars his entire life. He contacted this man, and the mechanic was happy to help him out. He took the car out on the road - Samie came along - and found some minor problems. Samie asked him to write down what these were, took the paper to the car dealer and said he expected these things to be fixed before he would accept the Ford. The dealer went along with everything Samie demanded. It was a most peculiar thing for Samie, to see this once pompous businessman taking orders from a poor student. It made him feel proud, and he grinned inwardly.

Two days later, he got a call from the dealer, saying the repairs had been done. Samie met with the old mechanic at the dealership, and the two men tried out the car again. When Mac was satisfied, Samie completed the deal. Then he invited Mac to lunch, at which occasion he heard a lot of interesting stories about cars and motors and carburetors and transmissions... Samie no longer felt incomplete.

One day, Samie discovered an ad in the newspaper in which his infamous dealership offered an Audi 100 for sale at the "special price" of the exact same amount for which Samie had bought it.

(Based on an actual event)

Elections

The elections of 2010 are over, thank goodness. Gone is the infernal propaganda that was enough to wean a thinking person permanently off television. I wonder if the sponsors have any idea that an overabundance of ads can be counterproductive.

The ads are gone, the mailings that served to burden the mail carriers and fill my trashcan have stopped coming, and only a few election posters are left on a few front lawns. Perhaps the owners didn't have time to put them away; or perhaps they're still gloating publicly for having had the wherewithal to pick the winning candidate.

That brings me to the winners of this or any other election. Like little children, they jumped for joy, if not in person then in spirit, for having won the game. Like the winners of a lottery, their smiles at their good fortune revealed much more than satisfaction; they were happy, elated, triumphant even, and underneath it all there was plenty of gloating. One candidate did not attempt to hide his elation; in full view of the public he did a summersault. Afterward, there were celebrations and congratulations and probably all sorts of partying that the public did not witness.

But why, I ask myself, are these "winners" so happy? They have to make plans now to move to the capital, at least part time, and families will be disrupted, and schools might have to be changed, and children and perhaps even wives or husbands will not be happy to have their well-ordered lives and routines torn asunder.

Why are these winners so happy? Don't they know that they have some very hard work ahead of themselves? It seems to me, they are actually the losers, because now they have to face dealing with high unemployment, the highly controversial health care plan, deficit and taxes, an enormous pile of debts, not to mention how to get out of Afghanistan, Iraq, and even Yemen without losing face. And how do we deal with Pakistan and its failure to head off the Taliban; and what about the longstanding feud between Israel and the Palestinians, and then there's Iran and North Korea, and on and on and on...

Why are they so happy, knowing that a crowd of contrary opponents is looming large and vociferous across the aisle? When Europe has elections, the winners appear very serious, downright somber even. They seem much more aware of the burdens of the office and the great and difficult work they are confronted with. But our politicians are overjoyed for winning. Could it be that some of them are so happy because they plan to do good things for the people? On the other hand, I'm sure that all are perfectly happy for having won total medical insurance coverage without having to pay for it! If I had that kind of benefit I, too, would jump for joy. As it is, I have to help pay for insurance coverage for that happy crowd even if I don't have enough income to buy it for myself.

But there must be more to their happiness than just insurance coverage. What else could be making them feel so very happy? There are two other benefits that come to mind: title and power. They have won grand titles that will bring them respect and perhaps even admiration, privilege and deference, but certainly the attention of countless fat-cat lobbyists and their highly welcome connections to money. And they have won, singly or collectively, great power, power to influence direction in national and international affairs, power to make their wills heard and felt, power to dictate to others, power to have their way.

But power corrupts, and we can see it verified throughout the ages, including the present time. Most unfortunate of all is the fact that those who are honest and incorruptible, who are devoted to the country and the nation and have only that in mind which serves the country well, can never be heard over the clamor of others who view political office as a personal step up – winning - on the ladder of success.

Riddle

Question:
What is the difference between the European hell and the European heaven?

Answer:
In the European heaven the British are the cops, the French are the cooks, the Germans are the mechanics, the Italians are the lovers and the Swiss manage it all.

In the European hell the British are the cooks, the French are the mechanics, the Germans are the cops, the Swiss are the lovers and the Italians manage it all.

Anonymous

Intermezzo

After the war was over
and the bomb craters had filled in
and the rubble piles had been cleared away
and the broken glass had been swept from the
sidewalks,

and before the German economic miracle
demanded the surrender of townhouse gardens
and tore away walking spaces to make parking
spaces
and replaced the star mosaic of cobbled sidewalks
with square slabs

There was sunshine.
It warmed the playground of the sidewalk,
filtered light through the leafy canopy of Linden
trees
It roused the scent of Linden blossoms
and threw quivering shadows that blurred the
cobbled images.
It gilded the curly heads of little children
who played with their dolls, and their scooters,
played catch and hopscotch and jump rope,
and the sound of their laughter adorned the still
afternoon,
while grown-ups withdrew to the cool seclusion
of their apartments above the shops,
resting in the twilight of dark green window shades
while life slowed down obligingly
and dozed in the tranquility
of days filled with sunshine.

In Praise of American Citizens

Countless Germans survived the firs years after the war only thanks to the food packages that came from the United States. This statement appeared in my hometown newspaper in 1996, fifty years after the end of World War II. It was one of a series of articles in remembrance of that period and what it was like to live in Germany at that time.

When World War II ended in Europe the continent was in chaos. Millions of people were on the move trying to get back to their home countries, fleeing or being evicted from their home countries, or trying to find a home since theirs was destroyed, or looking for lost relatives and family members, especially those who had served in the military.

The war ended for Germany on May 7, 1945 with a formal capitulation. During the previous months, January to May 1945, German civilians in the East began to take flight before the oncoming Red Army, and they headed West any way they could. Then followed expulsions and deportations of German populations from the Eastern regions until the end of 1945. Then, on January 28, 1946, Wladyslaw Gomulka, Deputy Prime Minister of Poland, announced the settlement of two million Poles in the eastern provinces of Germany. Poland demanded these provinces as payment and compensation for their own territory losses to the Soviet Union. With that, a new human wave was set in motion toward the West that would last another three years. Per month, one hundred and twenty thousand German civilians who were residing in the new Polish territory were to be deported to the West.

This decision by Gomulka became a permit for the abuse of Germans, to chase them out of their homes, to plunder their possessions and then ship the hapless wretches by freight cars to the West. Anyone who refused to submit risked his life or brutal torture and humiliation.

At the same time, the Tschechoslowakian government in Prag ordered Germans in the provinces of Sudetenland, Boehmen and Maehren to pack their bags and get out.

All these refugees or exiles descended on West Germany in hopes of finding a new home and a welcome reception. What awaited them, however, was a landscape of bomb craters and rubble piles. Germany had lost more than one third of its territories, agriculture had suffered enormously, industry lay in shambles. Feeding war survivors was difficult enough but near impossible once the refugees from the East arrived. In anticipation of that influx, German authorities, with the help of the Red Cross and other charitable organizations, had made plans for housing these people first in temporary collection centers, then around the countryside in villages and small towns. Apartment dwellers of any building that was habitable had to give up rooms to homeless people. My mother's sister, a farmer's wife, had to take in a woman with 2 children, another aunt had to give up a room to a single woman. My parents had too many children to give up any room. I remember a large group of small huts built in rows right next to our garden, the first one in an extensive community garden. One hut per family. When life began to improve, large apartment buildings with small units were constructed. By the 1960s, apartments for young married people were still hard to come by. Still, the people kept coming, escaping from the Russian occupation zone. Over the years, ever more and tighter fortifications were erected by East Germany along the border with the West, and between East and West Berlin, so that the number of escapees from Soviet domination eventually slowed to a trickle

Everything was in short supply at the end of the war, not just housing and food, but also teachers and plumbers and carpenters and men of all sorts of professions. My mother, in explanation of a question regarding the past, would often comment by saying, "there was nothing to be had." My family was fortunate because my father had business connections in the countryside; he knew many people and was held in high esteem by his acquaintances. While we surely faced shortages that I, as a child, knew nothing about, still, we always had to eat. I don't think we ever went hungry.

Besides housing, the most urgent need was food. While my family still had a house - although it had been damaged when a bomb hit the neighboring house - and had food, refugees and exiles were another matter. They were reduced to begging. On weekends the city dwellers went to the countryside in overloaded trains, on bicycles, on foot, any way they could, in the hope of finding something to eat. The country people did not have a whole lot for themselves and dreaded the influx of beggars. Their unusual dialects, dress, and behavior became a source of ridicule, and I remember well that we children, in our ignorance, made fun of them and their ways.

Eventually, soldiers returning from prisoner-of-war camps began to show up, begging for food. My mother always gave them something to eat; perhaps she hoped that her brother Ulrich, missing in action, would be treated equally well should he still be alive and on his way back. Much later she discovered why these soldiers always sought us out on the third floor, rather than begging from people on the first and second floor. It seems that the soldiers had an understanding. They left behind certain markings on the walls of the stairways, and the markings were designed to let other returnees know where food was made available. After our stairway was newly whitewashed the soldiers stopped coming.

Ten years after the end of the war prisoners were still returning from soviet prison camps. Among them was a physician who had taken care of his countrymen in the prison camp under the most primitive circumstances. He was hailed a Saint for his self-denial and total devotion to others.

Food had been rationed during the war, and the US occupation authority continued this practice in form of food stamps. Fifteen-hundred-and-fifty calories were allotted, "too little to live with, too much to die with" claimed a newspaper article. People became creative to survive. Those who lived at the outskirts of town grew vegetables wherever possible. Others managed to raise a pig and then butchered it – secretly, so that the weight of the pig would not be deducted from the food stamps.

Black market activities blossomed everywhere and even included American military personnel who wanted German money for going out with girls. And they were crazy for wine, the article mentioned, and traded three pounds of coffee for one bottle. We suffered a house search once when authorities, German and American, went through every room, the cellar, and the attic storage rooms. My father was then taken to the local jail where he was held for several weeks. The jail was located in the baroque guardhouse that was part of the city castle. It was located in a prominent part of town, and my father had to sweep the street around the building. It was a terrible humiliation for him. As an adult, whenever I asked about the circumstances of this event, I got different and evasive answers. An old neighbor of mine, an American woman of Italian descent, was right on when she laughed and said, "black marketeering; everybody was doing it." That's when I remembered the many leather purses of same style and color in our attic room. I had wondered why they were there. Without the black market hardly anything worked, and the request by the military authority to report any such activity remained unheeded.

"Countless Germans survived the first years after the war only thanks to the food packages for which American citizens donated through the private American organization

CARE (Cooperative for American Remittances to Europe.) CARE was established on November 27, 1945 by twenty-two charitable organizations in Washington D.C. The first CARE packages arrived in Bremen aboard the freighter "American Ranger" on July 15, 1946. The content of the packages was uniform; beside flour, coffee, tea, and other canned groceries they contained cigarettes and some kind of tablet for the purification of water.

About half of the packages were addressed to specific persons who had relatives in the U.S., the other half was available to any and all needy. Transportation and distribution, however, were a problem at first until the Red Cross and other such organizations became involved. The German Caritas Association even received a truck from the Americans to aid in distribution of the CARE packages.

Occasionally, CARE was beneficial in other ways as well. There was the case of a 28year old woman who was looking for a husband. She placed an ad in the paper with the statement that she had something to offer, namely a two-room apartment and every month two CARE packages. She received 2437 offers of marriage.

Smart Crow

I saw a crow come swooping down
A piece of bread it carried 'round
It settled on my bird bath rim
To quench its thirst by dipping in
Its beak, which held the dry old crust,
that fell into the water, drat!

But undismayed, the crow did drink
The water from my bird bath sink
And quenched its thirst, then took what was
the dry old crust now turned to mush
And gulped it down quite easily
I do believe, quite knowingly.

Nina, the Russian

From an article by Rudolf Kress in
"Buchenblaetter" Nr. 17, July 14, 2008

Growing up in post-war Germany of the 1950s, I sometimes heard my parents referring to someone by the name "the Russian," or "Nina." I vaguely knew that she had been maid in our household, and I remember Mother telling that she was an excellent artisan who had embroidered the white aprons we girls were used to wearing over our dresses. The aprons were of a style that covers the chest and has straps across the shoulders that tie with the waist straps in the back. They had decorative blue stitching around the edges, and at the top and bottom they had cross-stitch patterns that this maid had created totally from memory.

A child doesn't ask questions about matters that are outside its experience. Nina remained just a name, and since there was very little time for real conversation in my family I never had a chance to ask about her. Only very recently, when my oldest sister's husband, Rudolf Kress, submitted his memoirs of that time to a regional newspaper did I find out what Nina, the Russian, was all about.

The war started for Germany in September 1939 with the invasion of Poland. By 1941, the German military occupied large areas of Eastern regions, including Russia. Willing laborers for Germany were sought and found; they were needed to replace German men drafted into the military. But many Poles, Russians, and other nationals of the adjoining areas were forcefully transported back to Germany and forced into labor, mainly in the industries that supplied the war effort. German families too could apply at the employment office, which was responsible for the placement of the Russian women, for household help. Placement was granted to families with many children, or where the mother for health reasons could not attend the children, or mothers who had to work. The request for a Russian maid was first investigated for need. By 1942 my parents had six children under the age of six and were allowed to have a Russian maid. Her name was Nina.

The local branch of the National Socialist German Workers Party (NSDAP) warned families who obtained such a Russian maid against the dangers of maudlin political and racial sentimentality. Such behavior was considered damaging to the German racial and national honor. Repercussions for wrong behavior were threatened in a notice by the NSDAP on 2 Oct. 1942.

At that time, Rudolf Kress, my brother-in-law, was fifteen years old and employed as an apprentice in a local wax factory. The factory also employed twenty-five to thirty young Russian women in the production of candles. Their ages were between seventeen and around twenty-five, and they were collectively labeled "East Workers." The women were housed in company quarters in a building directly across the street from the factory. Several German employees and their families lived there as well.

In addition to sleeping quarters, the women had access to a large hall where they spent their free time. Some of the girls were excellent seamstresses; they always appeared well dressed in their off hours. However, the sign "East" always had to be worn visibly on their clothing.

Mr. Pit K., an employee of the factory, was responsible for the girls. They often came to him with their problems, and he always tried to do for them whatever was in his power. He even managed to obtain a sewing machine for the Russian women.

At the wax factory, Rudolf claims, the East workers were paid the same as their German counterparts received. They worked the same number of hours, had the same minimum income as German women, and like everyone else, they were enrolled in medical insurance and social security. Wages were paid out to them after deducting a sum for their room and board. They were generally not allowed to leave town, however, special permission was occasionally granted for a visit to a relative or friend who lived outside of town. The necessary travel pass had to be obtained by the employer from the local police station, and it had to be presented for the purchase of a train ticket.

It was part of Rudolf's job to pick up the paperwork from the women, pertaining to production and time cards. He was often received with the sound of melancholic Russian folksongs. The man who was in charge of that department, a Bible researcher and conscientious objector, had much compassion for these homeless girls. It was well known that he had spent time in a Nazi prison although he never talked about it. The danger of getting hauled off to prison again was too great. This man was also the company's fire marshal.

Every day around 11:30 am, one or the other of the company's two apprentices went with two of the Russian girls to the nearby kitchen of a local convent. They took along a hand wagon loaded with a large bucket for the food and a wooden crate to hold bread, jam, sausage, and a certain type of butter. This butter was packed like the regular butter but had less fat content and was apparently meant only for the foreign workers.

When girls complained of being sick, they were taken by an apprentice to the rubber factory which had a medical clinic staffed by doctors and nurses. The demand for medical attention was so great that if often took hours before they returned to the wax factory.

At holidays such as Christmas, Easter and New Year, the two apprentices of the wax factory, about fifteen years old, received greeting cards from the Russian girls. The boys never knew how the girls got hold of their addresses.

Few people had telephones, and most were therefore not publicly listed. The boys had mixed feelings about these attentions because it was strictly forbidden to have personal relationships with East workers. Some of the girls were very pretty and spoke fairly good German, and they were more open towards the boys than they were toward older co-workers. In time, they confided in the boys who had wanted to know why and how these girls came to be in Germany.

It happened when the German military had occupied their Russian hometowns for several months. One day, as happened from time to time, an order came from the German commander that all residents were to assemble at the town square. These orders were issued regularly for various reasons, i.e. the disbursement of food items or threatened reprisals for partisan activities. Severe punishments were announced for offences against regulations.

Men and women went, just as they happened to be, to the gathering place. They came in work clothes, aprons, in wooden shoes or felt slippers. All of them expected to return home within a short time. Suddenly, men in uniforms showed up and ordered the men to the right, the women to the left. Then they led the women out of sight to waiting trucks, and all women who were seen fit to work were loaded on to the trucks and driven away. No one was allowed to go back to their homes for any reason, not even to say good-by to family members. They were driven to collection points, and from there were transported via railroad to Germany; it was a very long trip. Now the boys understood why the Russians had arrived in Germany in such pitiful conditions. One of their first chores had been to take the women to the de-lousing station.

On Sundays, the boys could see the Russian girls out and about for walks with other East workers. The prescribed identification mark "East" was often deftly hidden under some clothing. The girls had to be back in their quarters at 10 pm. Despite these restrictions, two especially daring girls were sometimes seen waiting at the movie box office to buy tickets for the late show that would not be over before 11 pm. The boys did not report them. One evening, when the movie had sold out, the Russian girls sold their tickets to the boys.

It happened one day that Rudolf was told to bring Maria, the Russian interpreter and spokesperson for the Russian girls, to the director of the wax factory. He was usually a calm, rational man who was strict but always fair. That day, however, he was yelling so loudly at Maria that he could be heard through the door. It turned out that Maria was pregnant, and the boss, fearing for her, was nevertheless forced to report her to the authority. Eventually, Rudolf was called by the boss and told to take Maria to see a certain official at the employment office. In the office of that man, Maria was questioned in the presence of a translator, a young woman who had a Russian mother and spoke fluent Russian. After some hesitation, Maria named the father of her child; it was a French worker from the rubber factory. Had the father been German, his deed would have been considered by the Nazis as a degradation of the German blood, and reprisals would have been swift. Maria was soon picked up by the authorities most likely for the purpose of an abortion. Since she was needed in the workforce she was probably not punished but sent to a different worksite. She was never seen in the wax factory again.

During those years there was not much available for purchase because many goods, such as groceries, textiles, shoes, hardware, etc. were obtainable only with special coupons. Whatever income was available for fun and recreation was spent on movies, drinking, books, newspapers, picture postcard, postage stamps, etc. The East workers of the factory kept up a busy correspondence with other foreign workers within Germany. Mister Pit K. handed out the daily mail to the Russian spokesperson.

On September 11, 1944, an American air raid on my hometown, Fulda, destroyed the wax factory. All but one of the Russian girls were killed in the air raid shelter of that firm where they and other workers had sought refuge. On the morning of Easter Sunday 1945, American troops fought their way into our town. It had been the target of many air raids, was heavily damaged, and capitulated on the following day.

By the time the allies had overrun Germany there were between 6.5 and 7 million foreigners – called Displaced Persons (DP) – in the American, French, and British sectors of Germany. The majority of these civilians were former prisoners of the Nazi regime, forced laborers, and those who had willingly come to work in Germany and Austria. They were rounded up and housed in special temporary camps to await repatriation. By the end of 1946 nearly six million DPs had been repatriated to their home countries. For around one million people, going back to their homes in the Soviet occupied countries was not a solution. Among them were freed forced laborers, Jewish survivors who had lost everything in the East, and also East Europeans and people from the Baltic regions who had fought or worked of their own free will for Germany and feared reprisals on their return.

Feeding and housing that many people was a monumental task. The military authorities of the three Western occupied zones (French, British, American) enlisted the help of the United Nations' aid organizations. The greatest number of camps was located in the American sector; the last one was closed in 1957. There were no such camps in the Soviet sector, which became known as East Germany. The last camp in the British sector closed in 1959.

Have you seen this Lady?

She visited Portland, Oregon in early 2006

According to the Portland Art Museum, "*A Princely German Collection,* currently on view through March 19, 2006, is the Museum's most recent international exhibition. Organized by Mr. Buchanan and the Portland Art Museum in collaboration with the T.R.H. Moritz Landgraf of Hessen and his son Prince Donatus, the exhibition presents over 400 works of art drawn from the most important private art collection in Germany and includes Hans Holbein's Darmstadt Madonna. The Portland Art Museum is the exclusive worldwide venue for this exhibition."

Among the treasures was a famous painting by Franz Xaver Winterhalter who lived between 1805 and 1873. He was a farm boy from the Black Forest and grew to be European royalty's most favorite portrait painter. Queen Victoria, nicknamed "Europe's Grandmother," (the German Kaiser Wilhelm II, the British king George V, and the Russian Tsar Nikolaus II were her grandsons and first cousins to each other) called Xaver Winterhalter to her court where he painted the members of the many branches of her royal family.

The aforementioned painting is a portrait of Landgraefin (Countess) Anna of Hessen and princess of Prussia who lived from 1836 to 1918. When she sat for the artist she was 21 years old and had been married four years. It is a most beautiful, delicate, mesmerizing portrait of a beautiful woman.

I first saw this painting in its usual setting in castle "Fasanerie" which is in the private possession of the Princes of Hessen. It is situated just outside my hometown, Fulda, and has been turned into a museum. It also houses a lovely café with exit to a large terrace where visitors enjoy sitting on sunny days.

As is always the case when I view historical portraits – and I'm surely not the only one - I wonder what kind of people they were, what their lives were like, and what became of them.

When I discovered that the prince of Hessen would be sending a group of treasures from that castle to an exhibit in Portland, I went to see it. And there, again, I came across that portrait of the beautiful Landgraefin Anna of Hessen, princess of Prussia. I knew nothing about her, but thanks to books and papers that I have collected over the years, I know much more now than just her name.

Germany as it is today did not exist in the days of Anna. Countless little kingdoms and principalities, duchies and estates as well as church properties and free merchant cities were independent entities. They changed hands many times over the centuries, warred with each other, gained and lost property, overlords gave them as gifts for favors or took them away for punishment, and they became protestant or catholic according to the inclination of the new owner. Eventually, Hessen and with it castle Fasanerie were annexed by the kingdom of Prussia and thereby expropriated from the Hessen royalty. It happened during Anna's lifetime, and she was very hurt by this action. Seven years later, in 1873, Prussia returned several parcels of land and properties, including Fasanerie, as private property to Landgraf Friedrich Wilhelm of Hessen, and after his death to his widow, Anna.

Anna was born May 17, 1836 in Berlin, in the palace of her father, Prince Karl of Prussia. He was a younger brother of Prussia's king Friedrich Wilhelm IV, and he was also a brother of the later emperor Wilhelm I. Anna's mother, Maria, was the daughter of Grandduke Karl Friedrich von Sachsen-Weimar-Eisenach and the Russian princess Maria Paulovna. Anna's mother was also a sister of the future empress and queen of Prussia, Augusta Marie Luise Katharina.

Anna became the wife of Prince Friedrich Wilhelm von Hessen, a widower. The wedding took place on May 1853 in the chapel of castle Charlottenburg in Berlin. Anna gave birth to six children and experienced much unhappiness in her life. One of her children died at age ten. A few months later, her father died as a result of an accident. Two years later her husband died from a stomach ailment that he had acquired during a stay at castle Fasanerie. In 1886, her son-in-law died, two years later her eldest son died in Singapore from a tropical disease. Her second eldest son went blind as a result of an eye ailment. During WWII, 1914 through 1918, another son was injured and two grandsons died fighting for the Kaiser.

Her third grandson, Prince Philip of Hessen, born in 1896 became head of the Hessian house. In 1925 he married Mafalda, a daughter of the Italian king Viktor Emmanuel III. In 1943 Mafalda's father removed the fascist Benito Mussolini from the government. In response, Hitler sent eight divisions to Italy in an attempt to take over the government. Viktor Emanuel III was able to gain protection from the Allies for himself and his family. However, in an act of revenge Hitler had princess Mafalda arrested in Rom and sent to Buchenwald concentration camp. During a US bombing raid on August 24, 1944 Mafalda was gravely injured. Her arm had to be amputated and she died shortly afterward.

Anna was an unusually intelligent woman, a loving and affectionate mother and grandmother and a captivating person. She spoke several languages, had a large circle of friends and acquaintances and carried out an extensive correspondence. She was a skilled pianist and composed music. Johannes Brahms, Franz Liszt and Klara Schumann were among her friends. She dedicated herself to charitable works in military hospitals, for the poor and the unprotected. Fulda's cathedral, the catholic seminary and many religious orders were blessed by her generosity. The people of Hessen loved her very much.

The altar in the crypt of Fulda's cathedral holds the remains of St. Bonifatius, the "apostle" of Germany. He came to the area to convert the pagans to the Christian faith and start a convent during the 8th century. Every year, the catholic bishops conference takes place in Fulda, and during my youth there were countless religious observances and events throughout the year. A few Protestants lived around us as well, but they hardly registered in my mind. Only after coming to the US did I learn that Germany is primarily a Protestant country.

Countess Anna was by birth and marriage a Protestant. She was not only a Prussian princess and a Hessian Countess, she was also a member of the imperial house of Hohenzollern, also Protestants, of which Wilhelm II was the last German Kaiser. She had been drawn to the Catholic faith since her youth, and once she was widowed, in 1885 at age forty-nine, she often stayed in Castle Fasanerie. While there, she spent much time in Fulda with its cathedral and monasteries, convents and seminaries. its liturgy and art and all the beautiful events and services throughout the year. By 1901 she had made up her mind to join the Catholic faith despite her fear of creating political problems between the churches.

Her children respected her decision; they had known of her desire for a long time. Tensions between the Churches did not materialize, on the contrary, the Protestant church recognized Anna's inner conviction and therefore her right as a free person to choose her religion. All lay and church parties whose sanctions were needed agreed. But Kaiser Wilhelm II, head of the house of Hohenzollern, did not approve. Reference to other conversions, such as his approval for his sister Sophie to join the Greek Orthodox church when she married the Greek Crown Prince, did not change his mind. The Kaiser threatened Anna with ostracism from the house of Hohenzollern. Even before the actual conversion had taken place he began to address her formally with "your majesty," instead of the familiar "Du." The last sentence in a message read, "the house of Hohenzollern has ostracized and forgotten your majesty." Eventually, the Kaiser regretted his action and renewed contact with Anna shortly before he lost his throne in 1918 near the end of WW I.

Anna passed away that same year in her palace in Frankfurt on Main. Her remains were taken by train to Fulda, to be buried in the cathedral in a vault near her beloved patron Saint, St.Anna. Permission for a woman to be buried in the cathedral was granted by church and lay authorities, including Kaiser Wilhelm II. It was the first time that a woman was buried in the cathedral. It is a sure sign that Landgraefin Anna, Princess of Prussia, had been a most beloved Landesmutter (mother of the country) to the Hessians.

Sound Pictures

It was the sound that made me notice the silence on that still afternoon while strolling among honey locusts whose yellow-green foliage, delicate and lacy, filtered sunlight to the pavement. The inner One, emerging through my eyes, soothed lonely dogs that waited at the door, or by the stoop, or on the lawn, that accepted my attention with measured happiness because ecstasy was reserved for the master. And I stroked, no buried my hands in the exquisite softness of a cat whose want for human touch and affection had overcome its natural reticence. Squirrels tried to hide from me on runways that spiraled upward on trunks of huge firs, but my eyes could play that game too.

Suddenly, there it was – the sound that reached the ears of my memory and stirred up a sensation of pleasure. Shabble-de-clank, shabble-de-clank, getting louder as it came nearer, and when I looked up I saw a man on an old bicycle coming down the street, not quick like youngsters on their ten-speed bikes, but slowly, unhurried, like someone pacing himself for a long way to go on a plain old single-speed bike.

Shabble-de-clank went the old bicycle, and the sound painted a picture on the blank canvas of silence. With magic genius it scooped up from the depth of the unconscious all the other sound-pictures of life to relive, to re-enjoy, to deepen and broaden the present moment as with a multitude of footnotes.

Shabble-de-clank - and the blackbird trilled again in the reeds of the spring pond where I caught my first fish and thrilled to my new-found power. The water, ever receptive and willing, carried sound, pure and clear, in all directions. And I thought that if I were an artist I would pain the sky as blue silk, light and billowy, and I would paint the trilling sounds as pearls of exquisite sheen, rolling across smooth silk, each one embellishing the other.

Shabble-de-clank - and the meadowlark sang again on the fence post of the pasture on a tranquil summer afternoon and transformed the mundane job of hanging laundry to dry into a joyful excursion into a peaceful sanctuary. The deep blue sky encircled the earth, not separate and above but one with it. I wanted to reach up and pluck the bird song from the sky like an apple off the tree. The song hung in the air like a painting on the wall, a single painting on a large wall, undiminished by others, its impression enduring and immediate.

Shabble-de-clank - and the honking of geese, traveling the autumn sky in flying formation, evoked joie de vivre because the season of life and the season of the year I had lived to the fullest, and I knew the coming season to be no less joyful for the changes it would work. And I should never be sorry to see the seasons pass because there would always be another, like the trains I used to watch as a child, never knowing what kind they would be. Coming around the bend, slow and insignificant at first, exciting the senses as they grew larger and louder, speeding and roaring and then, at the peak of excited tension they whooshed past with a dizzying jumble of light and shade till the last car had whizzed by, following the others not to oblivion but only to another place.

The Fallacy of Free Time

Amid the entrepreneurial regards of our American way of life I dream of retiring from gainful employment, of sitting on my patio by the side of my favorite hemlock tree, surrounded by greenery to provide privacy from the neighbors, and filtered sunlight for my pleasure, no place I have to go to, sipping coffee, listening to the twitter of birds and the doodles of insects, books and typewriter on a table nearby. But since I need a house to accommodate my patio, and I need to eat in order to reach retirement age, earning a living is essential, and so I go about pretending to be a go-getter, a winner, a career-motivated fast-paced dynamic self-starter.

Tonight, though, I'm in luck. I have an entire evening to myself, quite by chance, and I wonder what exciting, unusual, stimulating thing worthy of unexpected free time I could do. It must, of course, have no resemblance whatsoever to anything even remotely connected with housekeeping. My youngest daughter is at a birthday party, and my youngest son went with his father to a basketball game, compliments of a friend. My eldest son is married, and so is my eldest daughter who has children of her own.

All right, now, what will I do? I could go to our wildly diverse and inexhaustible bookstore to rummage to my heart's content. But without money it wouldn't be much fun, and payday is two days away. I could go to the store and get some chocolate; but tomorrow I'll want to kick myself. How about writing letters? Lately, I've begun to suspect that my wrists are candidates for carpal tunnel syndrome; better give them a rest. Oh darn, I need to pack some things for the kids. After the basketball game, big brother will pick up little brother and sister to take them to his house to spend the night so that they can all go sledding tomorrow. They must have proper clothes if they are to enjoy the snow for any length of time.

There, that's done. It wouldn't have taken so long if little brother hadn't lost one of his good mittens and I had to find and mend his old pair. And then I discovered little sister's cache of outgrown sweaters. I must go through her things more often.

O.K. now, what is that exciting thing I'm going to do. Call a friend? I spoke to both of them today, and for a drink or dinner it's too late. A good TV show is always stimulating. Today is Friday, though, worst day for TV. - I better check the lights in the basement; the kids have a tendency to leave them on. -

Why do couples in sit-coms always wink at each other so suggestively when they discover that they have the house to themselves? I sometimes start to watch such a show, hoping that it would provide some pleasant entertainment after a busy day at work, to relax. But I can never take all that rubbish for very long, so I never find out what the winking is about.

I could listen to Wagner, but to properly appreciate such esoteric music I would want to read about it first. But I worked overtime today, all week, in fact, because my only co-worker was ill. I don't feel like reading. - Oh dear, I better get some laundry into the machine. With the dryer on the blink the basement clothesline has to make do, and it won't accommodate more than one load at a time. -

I would love to go to the library but it is closed. And I would love to go to a lecture but on Friday evenings nobody wants to give a lecture. I can't make cafe mocha, I don't have the gin for a pina colada, I don't want to call my mother because she always wants to know when I'm coming, and I hesitate to call my eldest daughter because I might disturb one of her few snatches of sleep between feedings of "general butterball" whose main occupation at the age of two months is eating. - Oh, there goes the telephone. -

That was a lady friend who, due to a medical condition, speaks very slowly, very detailed, and very lengthy, and I don't have the heart to cut her off. Now I still don't know what I'm going to do with that precious bit of time for my enjoyment.

Oh oh, there goes the doorbell. The kids are back.

Crows and other Pedestrians

Additional books by Rita Traut Kabeto

Call from the Past
a novel for young adults/adults, paper back

Fanny's Flight, sequel to Call From the Past
a novel for young adults/adults, paper back

Dagobert, second sequel
novel for young adults, adults, paper back

Tales from Bohemia by Pauline Bayer
translation of 20 stories about nature spirits and their
interactions with people, not sanitized, hand-bound in
cloth with a fairy motive.

Pigeon Hunts and other Pitfalls
a novel for the middle grades, paper back

When the Blackbird Called, poetry

Grimms Fairy Tales, Selected Stories
Translation of twenty stories from a third grade reader
in my youth in Germany, 20 stories wonderfully
integrated with landscapes, buildings and period
costumes, all from the state of Hessen

How the Mouse Spoiled Everything
a chapter book for children, paper back

Crows and other Pedestrians